IN HIDING

Tamina gasped.

She had a terrible feeling that the world was falling away beneath her feet and that she was about to faint.

She swayed and sat down abruptly at the desk in her father's big carved chair.

"Does Edmund – love you?" she whispered, wondering if perhaps there was still some reason to believe that this was all a dreadful mistake.

Edmund was an honourable man. He would never become engaged to one girl whilst in a relationship with another!

It was unthinkable.

"Of course he loves me! We are engaged. But I saw you dancing with him tonight and although Edmund assures me that you and he are just friends and that he escorted you to the ball because your parents are out of the country, I still felt that you should be told."

And with a click the connection was broken.

Tamina stared at the receiver in her hand, almost as if she did not know what she was holding.

THE BARBARA CARTLAND PINK COLLECTION

Titles in this series

IN HIDING

BARBARA CARTLAND

Barbaracartland.com Ltd

THE BARBARA CARTLAND PINK COLLECTION

Barbara Cartland was the most prolific bestselling author in the history of the world. She was frequently in the Guinness Book of Records for writing more books in a year than any other living author. In fact her most amazing literary feat was when her publishers asked for more Barbara Cartland romances, she doubled her output from 10 books a year to over 20 books a year, when she was 77.

She went on writing continuously at this rate for 20 years and wrote her last book at the age of 97, thus completing 400 books between the ages of 77 and 97.

Her publishers finally could not keep up with this phenomenal output, so at her death she left 160 unpublished manuscripts, something again that no other author has ever achieved.

Now the exciting news is that these 160 original unpublished Barbara Cartland books are already being published and by Barbaracartland.com exclusively on the internet, as the international web is the best possible way of reaching so many Barbara Cartland readers around the world.

The 160 books are published monthly and will be numbered in sequence.

The series is called the Pink Collection as a tribute to Barbara Cartland whose favourite colour was pink and it became very much her trademark over the years.

The Barbara Cartland Pink Collection is published only on the internet. Log on to www.barbaracartland.com to find out how you can purchase the books monthly as they are published, and take out a subscription that will ensure that all subsequent editions are delivered to you by mail order to your home.

NEW

Barbaracartland.com is proud to announce the publication of ten new Audio Books for the first time as CDs. They are favourite Barbara Cartland stories read by well-known actors and actresses and each story extends to 4 or 5 CDs. The Audio Books are as follows :

The Patient Bridegroom	The Passion and the Flower
A Challenge of Hearts	Little White Doves of Love
A Train to Love	The Prince and the Pekinese
The Unbroken Dream	A King in Love
The Cruel Count	A Sign of Love

More Audio Books will be published in the future and the above titles can be purchased by logging on to the website www.barbaracartland.com or please write to the address below.

If you do not have access to a computer, you can write for information about the Barbara Cartland Pink Collection and the Barbara Cartland Audio Books to the following address :

Barbara Cartland.com Ltd.
Camfield Place,
Hatfield,
Hertfordshire AL9 6JE
United Kingdom.
Telephone: +44 (0)1707 642629
Fax: +44 (0)1707 663041

THE LATE DAME BARBARA CARTLAND

Barbara Cartland who sadly died in May 2000 at the age of nearly 99 was the world's most famous romantic novelist who wrote 723 books in her lifetime with worldwide sales of over 1 billion copies and her books were translated into 36 different languages.

As well as romantic novels, she wrote historical biographies, 6 autobiographies, theatrical plays, books of advice on life, love, vitamins and cookery. She also found time to be a political speaker and television and radio personality.

She wrote her first book at the age of 21 and this was called *Jigsaw*. It became an immediate bestseller and sold 100,000 copies in hardback and was translated into 6 different languages. She wrote continuously throughout her life, writing bestsellers for an astonishing 76 years. Her books have always been immensely popular in the United States, where in 1976 her current books were at numbers 1 & 2 in the B. Dalton bestsellers list, a feat never achieved before or since by any author.

Barbara Cartland became a legend in her own lifetime and will be best remembered for her wonderful romantic novels, so loved by her millions of readers throughout the world.

Her books will always be treasured for their moral message, her pure and innocent heroines, her good looking and dashing heroes and above all her belief that the power of love is more important than anything else in everyone's life.

*"Whenever life becomes unbearable and your heart
is breaking, remember that love is just around the corner."*

Barbara Cartland

CHAPTER ONE
1911

The beautiful mirrored ballroom at Lord and Lady Mercer's vast mansion in Knightsbridge had seen many grand and exciting occasions, but none to rival the one in progress this warm summer evening.

The daughter of the house, Mary-Rose, was now eighteen and in honour of her birthday, her parents were throwing an extravagant fancy dress ball.

All the smartest and grandest members of London Society had flocked to the great house in a variety of marvellous colourful costumes.

Against Lady Mercer's better judgement, the band now playing up in the gallery that ran round the far end of the sumptuous oval room, had been imported especially from America.

In a side room tables had been laid with a sumptuous buffet. Ice statues in the shape of flowers stood between huge crystal bowls full of white roses and lilies.

Everything wonderful had been provided for the guests even champagne flowing down a pyramid of sparkling glasses.

Rumours abounded that there was to be a fire-eater

and a juggler later in the evening and a giant cake with eighteen candles.

Everyone was excited and happy and no one was more excited than Lady Tamina Braithwaite.

Small, slender and dressed in a quite amazing concoction of colourful chiffon and feathers, Lady Tamina had come to the fancy dress party disguised as a bird of paradise.

With a sapphire and emerald silk skullcap hiding her long blonde hair and a feathered mask covering her face, no one would ever have guessed who she was.

But beneath the mask, Tamina was bubbling with happiness as she was whirled around the shining parquet dance floor.

"Oh, Edmund, isn't this the most marvellous party you have ever attended?"

Edmund Newson smiled down at his partner. He had flatly refused to wear a fancy dress costume this evening – he had a dreadful fear of looking stupid, but his fair good-looks with a dapper moustache accentuating the handsome curve of his mouth more than made up for his reluctance.

"You are certainly the star of the evening, my dearest," he whispered as the music changed to a slow waltz and couples sank into each other's arms.

Tamina laughed.

"Oh, no, Edmund. Mary-Rose Mercer is the star and as it is her birthday, it is only right that she takes centre stage."

Edmund was concentrating on his steps and did not reply, but he knew that most eyes in the ballroom were following the quicksilver movements of the little green

2

and blue bird of paradise and not the heavier tread of the young girl dressed in the great white wig and cumbersome outfit of the ill-fated French Queen, Marie Antoinette.

Tamina closed her eyes for a few seconds, allowing the world to whirl round her.

She was so happy! She was in love!

Edmund was an up and coming politician. He had just won a seat in a by-election to the House of Commons.

Tamina had met him a month earlier when she had attended a race meeting at Ascot.

Her father, Lord Braithwaite, held a top position in the Foreign Office and on the morning of Ladies' Day at Ascot, he and Lady Braithwaite had quietly left the country on a diplomatic mission to Italy.

Although Tamina considered herself to be a girl with very modern ideas and outlook on life, she had been reluctant to attend the races on her own, but her elderly Godmother, Countess Lichley, who was very fond of her, had cheerfully agreed to be her chaperone.

But it had been an extremely hot day and after the buffet luncheon, the Countess had soon found a chair in a quiet corner and sat under her lace parasol to rest.

And the rest had turned into a long doze.

So Tamina had wandered around on her own and in one of the enclosures, watching the racehorses parading, she had been introduced to Edmund Newson by a mutual friend.

"Do you remember the day we met?" she whispered now as they circled round the ballroom, their colourful reflections changing every second in the myriad of mirrors.

Edmund nodded.

3

"Indeed, I do, little one. It is engraved on my heart forever as the most marvellous day of my life so far."

"Did you fall in love with me immediately?"

"Of course, sweetheart! Why do you think I asked you to marry me the following week?"

Tamina sighed.

It was all so wonderful. She felt like the heroine of a great romantic novel, swept off her feet by the good-looking and dashing hero.

Yes, she was engaged, but she had promised Edmund to keep their betrothal a secret!

Somewhere inside her head, a little voice whispered that her mother and father would be most upset to hear that she had been secretly meeting a young man and would soon be wearing his ring on her finger.

But Tamina pushed these doubts aside. Edmund was wonderful, so clever, so handsome, such a marvellous dancer and he loved her so much.

When her parents finally met him, she was sure they would love him too.

Tamina gazed up at his square ruddy face. Edmund was frowning – it made him look so sweet and serious. It was incredible to know that she was the most important person in all the world to him.

Tamina knew she was loved by her parents, but, as the youngest by far of three children, she had never attracted their undivided attention and affection.

Her two older brothers, Peter and Guy, had made the family a boisterous masculine place for a little girl to grow up in.

She had learnt to ride, to climb trees, to fall over and scrape her knees without 'blubbing', as the boys called her tears.

When they had finally departed for boarding school, she had missed them dreadfully.

She had several governesses who tried to turn her into a feminine frilly child, but every time Peter and Guy came home, they dragged their little sister into all their madcap schemes.

"I am so looking forward to introducing you, Edmund, to my brothers," she murmured as the music ended.

Arm in arm they walked out into the balmy moonlit garden and sat at one of the tiny tables scattered along the patio under flaring torches in bronze sconces.

"Ah, yes. They are both in the Services, I believe you told me? Away from home a great deal, I imagine?"

"Yes." Tamina felt tears prick her eyes for an instant. "Peter, who is the eldest, is in the Army and dear Guy, who always has to be different from his brother, joined the Navy."

"And do you expect them to be home on leave soon, my sweet?" enquired Edmund, kissing her wrist just above the edge of her gloved hand.

"No. Sadly not for months and months. By then I hope we can announce our engagement to everyone!"

Edmund's pale grey eyes looked sad.

"No one wishes for that more than me, Tamina. But as I told you, I am honour bound to tell my elderly grandmother first. She brought me up when my parents died and has the right to know our brilliant news before anyone else."

Tamina's eyes grew larger and bluer behind her feathered mask.

"And your poor grandmother is sadly very ill, you said?"

Edmund sighed.

"Yes. But her health is slowly improving all the time, so I am informed by her doctor. As soon as she is strong enough, you and I will travel to Scotland together and tell her our news. Until then, I fear we must keep our love a secret."

"But what – what if your grandmother does not get better?" whispered Tamina hesitantly.

Edmund patted her hand and stood up.

"Then we will marry immediately. Now I think some refreshment is in order. I believe ices are being served in the conservatory. Wait here, dearest, and I will fetch you one."

Tamina watched lovingly as he weaved his way through the dancing throng.

Then her attention was caught by a striking couple who were standing close to her chair.

She recognised the half-masked lady in the dark red dress as Lady Eunice Kenton. But the man seemed to be a stranger and Tamina was intrigued to know who he was.

He was attired in formal evening dress, but his face had been darkened and he wore a magnificent Arabian headdress with a fold that swept across his mouth so that only his eyes could be seen.

Even as she watched, Lady Eunice tapped his arm playfully with her feathered fan and walked away towards the stairs, the red silk of her dress swirling around her beautiful figure.

The man watched her go, then sank down onto a little gilt chair next to Tamina and sighed.

Ivan, the Earl of Daventry, felt exhausted, weary in every bone of his body.

It was hard to remember that only three months ago he had been living a happy-go-lucky existence in Italy, free of all worries and commitments.

As the younger son of the influential Daventry family, he had never needed to take on the duties and responsibilities as had his older brother, Geoffrey, who had been groomed to his position in Society from birth.

Ivan, five years younger, had wanted nothing more than to travel the world, learning about every country and the culture, the history and geography and backgrounds of the people he met.

His immediate plan was to write a book about all he had seen and learnt and then – if he had thought of the future at all, it had been vaguely that at some point he would probably go into the Diplomatic Service where his knowledge could be of use to his country.

Even when Geoffrey had inherited the title, he had not worried about what lay ahead for the Daventry family in the years to come.

His adored elder brother was happily married and his wife, Honesty, was carrying the new heir to the Daventry title. Everyone's lives seemed so happy and fulfilled. The future was rosy.

But all that had changed on a fateful snowy night in March when the carriage carrying Geoffrey, Honesty and their servants had overturned on a dark slippery road in the Lake District killing them all instantly.

It was hard now to even remember the last three months, he thought, closing his eyes against the whirling brilliance of the dancers in front of him. The pain and loss were still so great.

He was now the Earl of Daventry and his grief for his beloved brother and beautiful sister-in-law had to be kept under control, because there was so much to do and arrange.

Hurrying back across Europe at breakneck speed, he had been unable to believe the telegram he had received was true.

He had still half thought that it was someone's idea of a bad sick joke, but knew in his heart of hearts that no one could be that evil.

Then he had been forced to deal with the funerals, the grief of both families and the servants, as three of the family staff had died as well.

Next was to come the endless legal documents and complications to do with the estate.

He had felt the blackness of despair and exhaustion about to swallow him up until he had met Lady Eunice while out riding one day.

He knew nothing of London Society. Many of the older traditions and etiquette had been swept away with the turn of the century. The pace of life was much faster now.

He had been away from England for too long and had lost touch with all his friends.

Lady Eunice's brisk sympathy had been very welcome compared to the cloying affection of other acquaintances and he was now beginning to think that perhaps their new friendship might well blossom into something more lasting.

It was good to meet a girl whom he could trust so implicitly.

Loyalty and honesty were his first two requirements

8

for a lifetime companion.

Tonight was the first time he had ventured out into Society since the funerals.

Eunice had insisted that as it was fancy dress, he could attend without all the tiresome business of having to talk to people and listen to their sympathy.

But was he enjoying himself? The music was so loud, the colours so bright.

A few months ago, he would have thrown himself into the jollity, but now he looked back on that person as a different man.

The Ivan then was not the Ivan now.

He could not think clearly. He was so tired.

Just as he realised he had groaned out loud, a small hand touched his and he turned his head to find his neighbour's green and blue masked face turning towards him.

"Sir? Are you unwell? May I call someone to assist you?"

He stared at the brilliant feathered headdress and a smile smouldered in his dark eyes. As if this little thing could possibly help him!

The Earl had noticed her dancing earlier – a brilliant flash of colour against the paler pinks and creams of most of the other costumes.

Some sweet young girl at her first dance, he thought wearily. He nodded at her and Tamina thought, crossly, that she could see amusement gleaming in his dark eyes.

But it was hard to be sure because the bottom half of the headdress hid his mouth.

"I am scared to talk to you in case you fly away, little bird!" he said jokingly. "But please, have no concerns for me. I am in perfect health, although I must admit to being just a touch tired. And on that note, is it not long past your bedtime?"

Tamina frowned behind her mask.

She realised her lack of height and slim figure could make her seem young, but surely she did not appear of school age!

"I am glad you are not unwell, sir," she replied stiffly. "Are you enjoying the evening?"

"Very much."

"Your partner, Lady Eunice, is a wonderful dancer," added Tamina warmly.

"You are acquainted?"

"I have had the pleasure of meeting Lady Eunice, yes," she answered enthusiastically. "And her fiancé, Mr. Marshall. A very interesting American gentleman. Indeed, I believe he is over there at the moment. He travels backwards and forwards across the Atlantic all the time which must be fascinating. I would love to travel the world on a great ship."

"Mr. Marshall – ?" his voice sounded hoarse and Tamina wondered if her companion might be catching a bad cold.

She laughed lightly.

"He seems a very clever gentleman, but that is because he is much older than me. I believe he is nearly fifty, the same age as my Papa! I hardly understood a word of his conversation about bonds and finance when we met."

There was a silence and Tamina suddenly felt embarrassed.

Had she said too much about Mr. Marshall to a

complete stranger?

Her old Nanny always used to chide her for 'rattling on without thinking'. Oh, dear, had she been guilty of an indiscretion?

But surely Lady Eunice would have mentioned her fiancé before agreeing to dance with this gentleman in public?

Tamina knew that she would certainly mention Edmund to everyone, as soon as their secret engagement became common knowledge.

He pushed his chair back a little further into the shadows so she could no longer even see his eyes.

"But Mr. Marshall is a very kind considerate person, I am sure," she continued hastily, trying to make amends.

"I have not had the pleasure of meeting this Mr. Marshall," he said, trying to keep his voice steady.

Eunice engaged to be married! How could this possibly be? She would have told him.

No! This was insane. Why would a girl who was already engaged, pledged to a forthcoming marriage, enter into a close friendship with another man?

Where was her honour to her word? Where was her honour as a lady?

Obviously this girl in the blue and green mask had made a silly mistake.

She is very young and probably did not even know Eunice that well. She was tired – the hour was late and had muddled her with someone else.

Yes, that was what had happened.

But Tamina was speaking again and every word from behind the feathered mask dropped into his mind spreading like poison.

"I loved the story of how they became engaged on board ship when Lady Eunice was travelling back from New York. Her mother told my Mama that they were the only two people not affected by seasickness and one night they had the whole ballroom to themselves!"

The Earl stood up abruptly.

He could remember Eunice telling him when they first met that she had just returned from a visit to New York and that the voyage across the Atlantic had been terrifying because it was so rough.

She had even mentioned the empty dining room and ballroom. She just had not mentioned Mr. Marshall, her fiancé.

She had smiled and sympathised and lied to him for weeks.

But why?

That was the question his tired brain kept asking. Did she possibly imagine that an affair was what he himself wanted? Did he seem like that sort of man to her?

And what did other people in Society think? That he was the sort of blackguard that would seduce another man's fiancée when he was out of the country?

The Earl was quite well aware that because he had been living abroad and was not in touch with the news and gossip, it had been easy for Eunice to deceive him.

But other people would not see things in that light. No, he would be the villain of the peace and Eunice the sinned against victim.

And at that moment the Earl knew he would never trust a woman's words again.

He felt a fever sweep over him. After enduring such grief during the past few months, this betrayal was the final straw.

He made a distracted bow to the small elfin creature sitting next to him and strode away.

He did not want to face Eunice – he had no idea what he might say to her in this state of mind.

No, all he wanted was to go home and then get out of the country, as far away from Eunice as he could.

Tamina watched the stranger leave, then jumped up, determined to follow him.

She had the distinct feeling that she had somehow upset him by something she had said and knew she would not rest easily until she had discovered her fault and put it right.

Her old Nanny had often told her in the nursery,

"Never let the sun go down on your anger."

Well, this was not anger, it was guilt, but the sentiment was the same.

She walked swiftly round the outside of the house, weaving her way through the chairs and tables, past Emperors and Roman Legionnaires, Mermaids and Nursery Rhyme figures, all laughing happy couples.

The stranger had headed indoors into the throng of dancers. Tamina was quite sure that she could reach the hall where the staff would be fetching his cloak before he could battle his way through the crowded ballroom.

But as she rounded the corner of the house, she suddenly stopped, hesitating to take another step.

In the shelter of a doorway, she could see her darling Edmund talking to a tall thin girl in a plain green dress.

The girl was very pretty, Tamina noticed, with long brown curls that cascaded down her back from a complicated knot of ribbons.

But her dress was plain and rather shabby. Her only jewellery was a small silver cross worn at the neck.

Tamina could not believe that dressed in such a way the girl was actually a guest at the party. Perhaps she worked for the Mercers or had come to the house with a message.

She knew that Lady Mary-Rose Mercer had several small brothers and sisters, some of whom were still young enough to be in the nursery. This girl could well be their governess.

She started to walk towards the couple – and then hesitated again. They were standing very closely together. The girl's hand was on Edmund's sleeve in a pleading gesture.

Tamina bit her lip.

She had already apparently been less than discreet once this evening. She did not want to upset Edmund by interrupting a private conversation and the girl did look very upset.

Dear Edmund's expression was most solemn and concerned. Perhaps this girl had a problem and wanted him to help her solve it?

As a Member of Parliament, it was likely that he would often be asked for advice and Tamina felt that he would be cross if she interfered.

She turned and hurried the long way round the house, but knew in her heart of hearts that the stranger wearing the Arab headdress would have long gone.

The black and white marble hall was in fact deserted, except for a footman standing to one side, resplendent in the blue and red of the Mercer livery.

Tamina sighed. She would return to Edmund and

ask that he take her home.

The ball had lost its charm and interest.

Suddenly she felt very tired and was oddly unhappy that she would have no chance to undo whatever wrong she had inadvertently done to the dark-eyed stranger.

CHAPTER TWO

A candle burned in a little scullery leading off the vast kitchen of Daventry House in West London.

The room was dark and smelled of carbolic soap, the vegetable soup that had been cooked for dinner that evening and the rags the housemaids used to polish the brass fenders every morning.

But to the couple seated at the table, clasping hands on its rough white scrubbed surface, it was a haven of peace and happiness.

Joe Goodall, the Earl's valet, was only nineteen. He was far too young for such an important post, but like his Master, had been catapulted into his job when the former Earl had died.

Joe's older brother, Jacob, the late Earl's valet, had also been killed in the tragic coach accident.

Joe had been an under-footman at Daventry House at the time of the fatal crash, but at Jacob's funeral he had been approached by the new Earl and offered his brother's job.

He sat now, stocky and fair-haired, holding hands across the table with his sweetheart, Nancy Rider.

Joe had known Nancy since they were children and before he had entered the late Earl's service, he had lived in the same dirty rundown London street.

Nancy had lost her mother when she was ten and had to take over caring for her no-good father.

Bill Rider was a truly ghastly man, a contemptible bully who treated his only daughter worse than a slave.

"I must be goin', Joe," whispered Nancy, hearing the distant chimes of a Church clock. "Dad'll be 'ome from the boozer soon and if I'm not indoors with his dinner ready on the table, you know what'll 'appen!"

Joe tightened his grasp wishing he need never let her go. His beloved Nancy, seventeen, slim with long dark red hair that gleamed bronze in the candlelight. He loved her so much.

He glanced down at the pale skin showing at the edge of the long sleeve of her dress.

He could see the dark bruises and felt his blood boil.

Her father was a wicked brutal man and even more so when in drink.

"Why don't you let me tackle 'im?" he growled angrily. "I'll show 'im what for!"

Nancy shook her head.

"No! He'll 'urt you somethin' wicked, Joe. He cares for nothin' and no one."

"P'raps the Earl – "

Nancy pulled her hand away and stood up swiftly.

"No, Joe! Don't you even be thinkin' that. You'll get us both into dreadful trouble."

"Then we've only just one choice," he insisted stubbornly. "We 'ave to get wed! If we're man and wife, your Dad can't keep you at 'ome."

"But where would we go? What about your job?

We'd be out on the streets. We'd starve."

Joe stroked her cheek gently.

"No we wouldn't, sweetheart. I've got it all worked out. We elope to Gretna Green and get married, like I said. Then we'll come back, wait until the Earl's in residence down at Daventry Hall and ask him for employment."

Nancy's lips trembled. She was a brave girl, but had never met the new Earl.

"Why would he 'elp us if you'd already left 'im without givin' notice? You wouldn't even get near enough to speak to 'im. Some old butler would have you thrown out on your ear."

Joe bit his lip.

"The Earl's a good man, Nancy. A fair man. I know 'e is. Jacob always spoke so 'ighly of him. I'm sure he'll understand."

"Oh, Joe, to be your wife, to be together for ever. That would be a dream come true!"

They clung to each other for a brief moment and then Nancy pulled away.

"I must go. It's getting' so late."

Joe helped her on with her cloak.

"My Master is plannin' on goin' down to the country in two days' time. I'll come for you and we'll catch the coach to Scotland. By this time next week, you'll be Mrs. Joseph Goodall! I swear!"

At that moment there came the sound of a bell ringing violently through the still house.

"That be the Master back from the Mercers' Ball. He's early," Joe said. "He'll be wantin' coffee or a whisky, I expect. I'll 'ave to go."

And dropping a quick kiss on Nancy's soft lips, he watched her tenderly as she slipped out of the scullery door into the night.

*

In a great house in the centre of London, another young girl was slowly preparing to retire for the night.

Tamina had arrived home early from the ball.

She had pleaded a headache to Edmund and felt guilty when she saw how concerned he was for her welfare.

Dear, sweet Edmund. How happy they would be when they were finally man and wife.

She had been unable to explain to herself why the ball had so suddenly lost its appeal.

The dark-eyed stranger wearing the Arabian style headdress had unsettled her. And she had felt most uncomfortable watching Edmund talking in the garden to the tall girl in the shabby green dress.

It had almost felt as if she was intruding, which was ridiculous because Edmund was her fiancé, even if their engagement had to be kept a secret.

Tamina picked up the card that had been attached to the huge bouquet of pink and white roses that Edmund had sent her earlier in the day.

"I love you, I adore you, I worship you and these flowers come to you from my heart. They are beautiful, but not as beautiful as you!

Bless you, my darling, and I am counting the hours and the minutes until I can be with you."

She had read the letter a dozen times and finally kissed it before she tucked it away in her reticule, remembering her promise to Edmund that no one should

19

know what was happening until he could tell her their love was no longer a secret.

Tamina had dismissed her maid for the evening and now she unhooked her blue and green fancy dress.

'This little bird of paradise is going to bed,' she said softly to herself with a laugh.

She was sitting in front of the dressing table mirror, wearing her favourite old red velvet dressing gown, brushing out her long fair hair, when there was a tap at the door.

"Come in!"

She turned wondering who on earth could be disturbing her so late.

"Miss Tamina – " It was Angus, one of the footmen on duty. "There is a telephone call for you."

Tamina stared at him in astonishment.

"A telephone call for me?" A cold chill ran over her body. "Is it my Papa? Has something awful happened?"

Angus, who was very fond of Tamina as he had known her since she was a child, shook his head. He knew he should feign ignorance, but he hated to see the distress on the beautiful face before him.

"No, it is a young lady, miss, who urgently requires to speak to you. I took the liberty of saying that you had retired for the evening, but she insists it is vital she speaks to you tonight."

Tamina stood up and tightened the cords of red velvet round her slender waist.

"Very well, Angus. This is all most strange, but I will come downstairs at once."

The telephone stood on the desk in her father's imposing study.

Tamina had not used the telephone too often as she saw most of her close friends every day and had no need to speak to them except face to face.

She spoke hesitantly but clearly.

"Hello? This is Tamina Braithwaite. How may I help you?"

"I must speak to you," said a girl's voice, "because I want to tell you the truth and the truth is what I think you should hear."

"The truth about what?" asked Tamina, bewildered. "Are you certain you have the right person? This is the Braithwaite household."

"You are exactly the person I want to speak to," the voice replied dramatically. "I want you to realise that what I am telling you is the truth and nothing else."

"The truth about what?" demanded Tamina again, wondering if the caller was perhaps unwell.

"I understand," continued the voice, "that you are great friends with Edmund Newson."

Tamina drew in her breath sharply and her fingers twined nervously around the telephone wire.

"How does that concern *you*?"

"It concerns me," came the reply, "because for over a year he has been in love with me. We are engaged and he has promised that the moment he can afford it, we will be married."

Tamina gasped and then she stammered,

"I – d-do not – understand."

"It's not difficult," said the girl, a sob breaking through her words. "Edmund has very little family money. He cannot afford to marry for love and he finds it very difficult to be with me as much as he wants to and so we have to keep our engagement a secret."

She paused for a moment before continuing,

"I have a job and we are saving every penny we have. I am asking you, begging you, please do not encourage him to leave me! You can have any man you like! You are rich and pretty. *Please* leave Edmund alone."

Tamina was listening, although the roaring sound in her head was drowning out the words.

This could not be her Edmund this girl was talking about.

In a voice she hardly recognised as her own she enquired tentatively,

"Do you mean Edmund would marry you if he had sufficient funds?"

"*Of course* he would," the reply came simply down the wire. "He has been my lover for over a year now. We see each other whenever we can, but even with his new position in the House of Commons we cannot afford to marry. Our future depends on Edmund making a great deal of money."

Tamina gasped.

She had a terrible feeling that the world was falling away beneath her feet and that she was about to faint.

She swayed and sat down abruptly at the desk in her father's big carved chair.

"Does Edmund – love you?" she whispered, wondering if perhaps there was still some reason to believe that this was all a dreadful mistake.

Edmund was an honourable man. He would never become engaged to one girl whilst in a relationship with another!

It was unthinkable.

"Of course he loves me! We are engaged. But I saw you dancing with him tonight and although Edmund assures me that you and he are just friends and that he escorted you to the ball because your parents are out of the country, I still felt that you should be told."

And with a click the connection was broken.

Tamina stared at the receiver in her hand, almost as if she did not know what she was holding.

Carefully she hung up, concentrating because her hand was trembling so much.

Beyond the yellow circle of light from the desk lamp on her father's desk, the room was dark.

The shelves of leather bound books seemed to close in around her. The marble busts of great statesmen and Greek Gods that stood in shallow alcoves seemed to be sneering at her.

Tamina gazed into the swirling shadows, knowing that never again would she enter this room without feeling a surge of deep despair.

What she had heard could *not* be true!

Yet in some odd instinctive way she was certain that it *was* true.

She realised that she had always suspected in some recess of her heart that Edmund was attracted by her family and position in Society.

He asked so many questions about her father and mother and which important people in the political and artistocratic world came to the house for dinner parties or meetings.

She knew he expected to be included in that way of life very soon and when they were man and wife that is just what would have happened.

But to marry her when he loved someone else! How could he have condemned them both to such a barren life together?

Tamina felt the first tears gather in her eyes and run unheeded down her cheeks.

It was now becoming clear why he had insisted on their engagement being kept a secret.

Was there even a sick old grandmother living in Scotland or was that a lie too? Probably. He had been scared that this other girl would hear of their relationship and cause a scene in public, which would be ruinous to his political career.

Tamina was quite sure that she was the girl she had seen talking to him at the ball.

Everything now made a terrible mind-wrenching sense.

"Oh, Edmund! How could you do such a dreadful, dreadful thing?" she whispered out loud.

She now recognised that if their wedding had taken place, he would still in his heart be desiring the girl he loved and who had worked so hard to provide money so that they could be together while apparently he could not afford to marry her.

It was the first time in her life that Tamina had ever thought of her money or position in Society as causing difficulties or being an attraction that men would find irresistible.

If she had ever considered the fact that they were rich, she had seen her father's money as something which enabled them to go abroad whenever they wanted. To travel on the best ships and stay in the best hotels.

Her father was wealthy and undoubtedly his important position at the Foreign Office meant that everyone wanted to know him and receive the invitations he and her mother sent out practically every week of the year.

They invited guests to dinners, balls, weekends in the country at the Braithwaite estate in Devon, boating parties on the river, outings to the races and anything else fashionable in the appropriate season.

Tamina had received a great deal of attention since she came out in London Society. She believed, in her innocence, that men liked her for herself.

Now the scales were falling from her eyes.

'It is not me the men are running after,' she told herself, 'it is my father's fortune. If I was as plain as a pikestaff and as badly dressed as some women are, even badly educated, they would still be knocking on the door and inviting me to dance with them. Eventually, like Edmund, they would ask me to marry them.'

She wanted to scream because it was all so humiliating.

Worst of all was the fact that she had stupidly believed all the compliments she had received.

She had thought the men who said she was adorable were thinking of her and not her money.

What was more the reason why she was invited to so many parties was not because they wanted her company, wanted to hear her views and opinions, get to know her as a person, but because they wanted access to her father.

'How can I bear it? How can I live with this knowledge?' Tamina howled at herself.

But for the moment there was no answer, only the

darkness which seemed to her the darkness of humility and misery.

Edmund, the man she loved so much, had betrayed her in every possible way.

"What shall I do and what shall I say to him?" she asked out loud to the uncaring marble busts that stared sightlessly down at her. "How can I live now I know the truth?"

But there was no answer and she felt as if she had suddenly entered a new world of shadows where, at the moment, there was no light.

*

In the West of London the Earl of Daventry tore off his evening jacket and threw it carelessly onto a chair. The remains of his Arabian headddress had been discarded long ago.

He kicked the smouldering logs in the grate, but only a few sparks leapt up the chimney.

He rested one hand on the marble mantlepiece and gazed down into the ashes in despair.

Ashes – that just about summed up his life.

Eunice was already engaged to be married! She had lied to him. Well, perhaps not in so many words, but surely, "are you free to be my close friend?" was not a question any gentleman would have needed to have asked a young lady.

Why had she not told him about the American, Marshall, when they first met? It was so astounding that he still could not quite believe it.

But what if the young girl at the ball had been wrong? She was no more than a child and children often see things from a mistaken point of view.

26

He kicked at the smouldering logs again, finally extinguishing all life.

No, there was no hope. Once she had told him, one or two other little moments, some casual remarks from acquaintances began to make sense.

And that was what made it so much worse! Not that a woman had taken him for a fool – that could happen to any man who lived life to the full, but that his honour and standing in Society were now threatened.

People would be talking and gossiping behind his back. He could picture the scene – the silences that would fall when he entered a room and the dry remarks from fellow members of his Club.

He would be cast in the role of 'the other man', someone who would blatantly attempt to break up an engagement and – what was even more bitter to the taste – while the lady's fiancé was not even in the country to defend his relationship.

Well, he decided he would not stay here in England a second longer!

A gentle tap at the door made him start.

Joe, his young valet, entered carrying a pot of coffee on a tray.

For a second the black clouds around him lifted. The boy looked so serious, his fair hair falling into his brown eyes, concentrating on carrying the heavy load without tripping.

The Earl could not recall Joe's brother, Jacob, who had also been killed in the appalling accident that had changed so many lives. But he knew from family letters that he had been a fine young man and he was sure that Joe would follow in his footsteps.

"Thank you, Joe. That is most welcome."

"Do you wish me to light another fire, my Lord? I had one lit earlier because it seemed a little chilly even for a summer night."

"No, Joe. That will not be necessary. But Joe, there is something you can do for me."

"My Lord?"

"Start to prepare my clothes and yours for a long trip. As soon as I possibly can, I intend to take passage by sea to somewhere far away. And you will be coming with me."

*

Tamina was pacing round and round her bedroom, trying to stem the tears that were burning her eyes.

'I must go away. I can't stay in London. What will I say to Edmund when we meet? Oh, I hate him! *I hate him*! But I love him, too!'

She flung herself on top of her bed, burying her hot face in the cool lavender-scented pillows.

'Oh, if only Mama was here with me. I could explain to her, tell her. She would understand.'

She wondered briefly if she could travel out to Italy to her parents, then knew with a sinking certainty that she could not.

Her father was on official, if discreet, Foreign Office business and her mother was there to help and officiate at all the luncheons and dinner parties they would be giving and attending.

Although it looked as if they were only in Italy to enjoy themselves, Tamina knew that Lord Braithwaite would, in fact, be deeply involved in very delicate political negotiations.

The arrival of a distraught daughter talking about a secret engagement that was no longer happening because she had been betrayed by a dishonourable man would not be helpful.

She could not impose such a burden on her dear parents.

Tamina rolled over and stared up at the ceiling. She rubbed at her eyes with a wisp of lace that was soaking wet.

"Oh, Edmund. What have you done?" she cried helplessly and miserably feeling that her whole world had fallen to pieces.

She had felt so happy that she was flying up into the sky.

Her love for Edmund had increased not only every time she met him, but every day and every night she loved him more and more.

As she tossed from one side of the bed to the other, she kept thinking that everything he had said to her was completely untrue.

When he had said he loved her more than anyone else in the world, he was really thinking of the other woman he loved and not her.

Slowly she sat up.

She would not stay in London to be embarrassed by having to meet Edmund and tell him she had discovered his unscrupulous duplicity.

Now, when Tamina thought back, she really could understand why he had made all he had said to her so convincing so that not for one moment did she suspect his words were anything but the truth.

What he was really saying was,

"I love your money and position in Society. I want your money and I must have your money and be accepted by the circle of people you are part of. With all that I will be more important in every way than I am at the moment."

'That is what he really desires,' Tamina told herself. 'I have been fool enough to believe that I mattered more to him than anything else in the whole wide world."

For an hour she dozed fitfully and then as dawn started to show apricot and peach shades in the Eastern sky, she woke and began to bathe her face in cool water.

'How do I face him?' she asked her pale reflection. 'How do I cope in the days, weeks and months ahead with this misery in my heart and soul? How can I make him realise I know the truth and that his words of love which seemed to lift me into Heaven itself were merely a pretence or rather a way to grab my father's money to make his life successful?'

Suddenly she knew she could not face Edmund.

It would be impossible to listen again to his words of love when they were all lies.

Lies which he told so cleverly that she believed everything he said to her.

'He will tell me that I am mistaken and that the girl on the telephone was the one who lied. And every word he speaks will drive another nail into the coffin of our love, because it will show me over and over again that he has no honour.'

Tamina rubbed at her lips with a cloth, trying to erase the mere thought of Edmund's kiss.

She had felt when he kissed her that he not only gave her his lips, but his heart and his very soul.

But all he had given her in reality was a taste of *hell*.

CHAPTER THREE

For Tamina, the next day passed in a haze of misery.

She stayed in her room, informing her staff that she had a bad headache and was definitely not at home to anyone, including Mr. Newson.

Flowers arrived from Edmund. One delicate posy of violets and tiny white rosebuds at noon and later in the afternoon, a huge bunch of lilies and gardenias bound with yards of pink ribbon.

Each offering was accompanied by a fulsome note, expressing his warmest love, his deep regret that she was ill and hoping upon hope that she would soon recover.

Tamina read the hand-written lines, the declarations of never-ending love and felt a surge of anger mixed with despair.

How dare Edmund write such words when he was engaged to another woman?

It was diabolical behaviour.

Twenty-four long hours passed.

Tamina could not sleep, could not eat. All she could think of were the shattered dreams that lay all around her.

And she was now facing her biggest problem. She could tell no one and even her brothers were both abroad in the Army and Navy.

If Peter and Guy had been at home, they would undoubtedly have been furious with Edmund and there might even have been a fight, because, as much as they bossed her around, she was still their little sister and would be horrified at the thought of someone hurting her.

But as her engagement to Edmund had been such a secret, even her best friends had no idea that she had lost her heart and had it broken, all in such a short space of time.

Her closest friend was the youngest daughter of the Duke of Marlow. If only she had told Charlotte about Edmund, she could have gone to stay with her and her family on their vast Yorkshire estate. Edmund would never have found her there.

Now she knew what she had to do. Get away from London until she was fully recovered.

She could not cope with some dreadful scene with the man she loved so much.

'I cannot stay here,' she mumbled to herself. 'It is far too easy for him to contact me. At some point one of the servants will let him into the house or he will lay in wait for me in the street! Oh, it will be *too* dreadful.'

What could he possibly do or say to put things right between them? In the dark hours of the night, she had run through various silly conversations in her mind.

'Oh, Tamina, my love, of course it is you I adore. This girl is deranged. She has recently been in a mental institution and has been tracking me, pretending to be my fiancée.'

No, it was all rubbish.

He had behaved dishonourably because she was rich

and her father was Lord Braithwaite.

Tamina knew that she would never *never* forgive Edmund.

If she ever found peace of mind again, then she could return to London and just tell him, calmly and dispassionately, exactly how she had felt and how ashamed he should be of his behaviour.

She tossed and turned in her bed, trying to find a cool place on the pillow for her head.

'Yes, I will go away, but not just on a holiday as Lady Tamina Braithwaite. Even if I travel people will know who I am. They will know I am rich and my parents are important. How will I ever discover if they like me for myself?

'I will always be thinking that people want to speak to me, be in my company, just because of who I am and what my family own.

'No, I must now go in disguise, take a job and find something to do so that no one will guess who I am. I must do something new and exciting to take my mind off the unhappiness I feel now.'

Tamina climbed out of bed and knelt on the window seat, gazing out at the beautiful moonlit garden beneath her. The colourful flowers were all bleached to white and silver in the moonlight, but she saw none of them.

She ran through her talents in her mind.

'I have been well educated – better than many girls thanks to Papa's modern views on women. I can teach children and be a governess or perhaps a companion to an elderly lady. Or I could offer my services as a secretary.'

Tamina knew that she still had the skills she had acquired at her finishing school in Switzerland, even if they were a little rusty.

Some of the girls who had been in Geneva with her had thought it very odd that she, Tamina Braithwaite, should bother to learn such mundane things as typing and how to take dictation.

"But Tamina, you are so silly!" they had exclaimed. "Why are you still bothering your head with that dirty typewriter and all those horrid little squiggles? You'll never need to do either of these boring tasks once you are home and have come out!"

But although she had not enjoyed her lessons, Tamina had persevered. Her father had mentioned to her that one day, when he had retired from the Foreign Office, he would like to write his memoirs.

He had enjoyed such a full and interesting life and could tell stories and anecdotes about so many famous and important people.

But because of the confidential nature of the papers he would be consulting, he thought it would be useful if Tamina could help him instead of employing a secretary who might not be so discreet.

Tamina crawled back into bed.

Yes, that was what she would do. She would find a job and leave England and Edmund behind her.

Even making the decision made Tamina feel a little better.

By the time the sun was shining into her bedroom, she had washed and dressed hurriedly, putting on her plainest outfit, a dark green skirt and jacket with black piping on the collar and cuffs, worn over a plain white blouse with very little decoration.

She did not bother to call her maid, but pinned up

her long fair hair into a tight knot herself.

There! Now she looked like a severe hard-working girl.

'And I know exactly where to go to find a position,' she whispered to her reflection in the long cheval mirror. 'Mrs. Shepherd's Employment Agency!'

She ran downstairs into her father's study. Even though he was away, the butler solemnly laid out the morning newspapers on a side table every morning.

Tamina had believed that she would never enter this room again without feeling waves of despair, but she was so engrossed with her plans that she only felt a twinge of pain when she caught sight of the telephone that had brought her so much grief.

She picked up *The Times* and turned the pages to the advertisement section.

Mrs. Shepherd's Agency was the place where the Braithwaite's housekeeper always went for staff. She would interview several suggested by the Agency and Tamina's mother would make the final selection.

But Tamina knew they all said the same thing when asked.

"I have been sent by Mrs. Shepherd, my Lady."

Holding up the newspaper she read the column, "*Mrs. Shepherd requires.*"

There was a long list which began,

"*Outstanding and experienced cook required by a gentleman and lady of political importance. Must be experienced in French cooking as well as English.*

Experienced nurse is required by a lady who is suffering from an illness which prevents her from walking."

A butler was sought for a house in the country. Experience essential.

A lady's maid for someone in London and a nurse for the yet unborn child of an Italian Contessa.

Then almost at the bottom of the page Tamina read,

"*A secretary is required. Must be prepared to travel abroad immediately and for some time. Knowledge of French, Italian and Portuguese an advantage.*"

Tamina read it once and then again.

Well, she was ready to travel immediately. She could speak both French and Italian and knew a little Portuguese because several of the girls at her finishing school had come from that country and she had enjoyed talking to them in their own language.

She was quite certain that it was worth her while trying to obtain this position.

This was her chance to escape from England and Edmund!

*

Ivan, the Earl of Daventry, paced back and forth in his study at Daventry House. The butler had just shown out another useless applicant for the position of secretary.

'Silly woman!' he muttered to himself. 'I have no time for these Society girls who have never worked a day in their lives and think that this job is just an excuse for a cruise in the sunshine!'

He was in a fever of impatience to leave England.

He had already booked cabins on a ship leaving Southampton in two days time bound for the Island of Madeira, but he could not set out on his great venture without a secretary.

'I just need a good hard-working, but well-educated girl who will take down the notes I give her and type them up for me. Someone who has a knowledge of languages and will not be frightened by travelling abroad! Surely it isn't that difficult for Mrs. Shepherd to find me such a person?'

The Earl flung himself down in his leather chair. He knew in his heart of hearts that he was being unreasonable and irritable, but still running through his mind was the constant knowledge that Eunice had betrayed his trust.

'Society women!' he mumbled. 'I shall have nothing more to do with any of them. They are all the same, just out for a good time, going to dances and parties, breaking hearts left, right and centre without any thought for the consequences.'

Just then a knock at the door heralded Cobham, his butler, who announced the next applicant,

"A Miss Waites from the Agency to see you, my Lord."

The Earl looked up, unaware that he was glaring, then his dark gaze softened.

He was looking at a small slim girl wearing dark green. Her hair – what showed under an incredibly ugly green hat – was very blonde and she had the biggest blue eyes he had ever seen.

She was incredibly pretty, but also looked extremely sad. He wondered briefly if she had suffered a recent bereavement.

He stepped forward and shook her hand.

"Miss Waites?"

"Yes, my Lord. Ta-Tabitha Waites," said Tamina, flushing as she stuttered over the false name she had given to Mrs. Shepherd at the Agency.

"Please sit down, Miss Waites."

He watched as she seated herself primly in front of his desk.

He perched on the edge of his chair, his restless fingers playing with the heavy silver letter opener.

Miss Waites looked up at him and he was glad to see there was no sign of fear on her face, nor the simpering silliness that had been so apparent in the last girl's expression.

"Did the Agency explain what I needed, what the job entails?" asked the Earl.

"Yes, indeed. They told me that you are soon to travel abroad, that you are writing a book and need a secretary to take care of your notes and help in any way she can."

The Earl glanced down at the papers she had handed him.

"I see here that you have you recently worked as secretary to Lord Anglesey?"

Tamina crossed her fingers under cover of the handbag she held on her lap.

She was about to tell a lie, but hoped this childish gesture would exonerate her!

Lord Anglesey had, in fact, been her Godfather; a very elderly nobleman who had lived in a rundown castle in the wilds of Wales until his recent death.

Tamina knew that his real secretary, a lovely lady called Miss Holder, had retired with a pension to a tiny cottage on the castle estate.

Tamina was taking a great risk, but was fairly certain no one would ever have known whom Lord

Anglesey's real secretary was.

"Yes, my Lord. I'm afaid that I do not have a written reference from him, but I can assure you I am used to dealing with all sorts of difficult handwritten notes and taking dictation. I am very discreet but have opinions when consulted."

"You speak French and Italian?"

Tamina smiled.

"*Mais, certainment!*"

The Earl looked up sharply.

Was this slip of a girl checking that he himself understood her? But her face was still very composed, although there was a sparkle in her blue eyes that he found appealing.

He wondered at the sadness he could see in her face.

Surely it could not be for her late employer? Lord Anglesey had been well into his eighties, if his memory served him correctly.

"And you have no concerns or problems with leaving England immediately? No family claims that might prevent you staying away for some months?"

Tamina shook her head.

Oh, to be away for weeks from Edmund. It sounded too good to be true.

"Well, you will be travelling by ship to Madeira with me and my manservant. I have booked the cabins and obviously your salary will include all meals and an allowance for some summer clothes as it will be very hot where we are going."

Tamina nodded.

She was impressed by the Earl. She liked his down-to-earth manner.

He was certainly a very good-looking man with dark hair and eyes, but his face was pale and strained as if he had not slept well for several nights.

She knew from Society gossip that the Earl had inherited his title when his brother and sister-in-law died so tragically.

She could recall her parents' shock at the dreadful news. They had only met the late Earl and his wife once, but it was always appalling to hear of such a devastating accident.

Tamina decided the Earl was still grieving, although the coaching accident had taken place several months earlier.

And it was odd sitting here gazing into his dark eyes, noting that his black lashes were absurdly long for a man.

She had the feeling that she had met him somewhere before, although she knew she had not.

"May I ask, my Lord, what type of book you are planning to write?"

The Earl's grave face suddenly looked warmer, more approachable.

"It is to be a history and travel book combined, Miss Waites. Most authors write either one or the other. But I have lived abroad for many years and I think it would be useful to write a book that combines not only information about different countries, but about their history as well.

"I intend to begin by documenting the history and aspects that travellers would find of interest on the Island of Madeira."

Tamina now clasped her hands together, her eyes sparkling.

"Oh, that does sound *so* interesting and it is why you advertised for your secretary to have a knowledge of Portuguese. Most travel books just tell you which excursions to take or the temperature at certain times of the year. I have often wondered how society runs in say, Italy, when I am there."

"So you have travelled to Italy, Miss Waites?"

Tamina bit her lip.

She had almost given the game away! She would have to be far cleverer than this if she was going to fool the Earl.

"Well, yes, I went to Rome with an older lady two years ago," she told him, which was not even a lie, as she had gone with her dear Mama who was definitely an older lady!

She paused for a moment to recover herself and added,

"I would be thrilled, my Lord, to help you with such a worthwhile project."

The Earl felt a little of his heaviness of spirit lift at the young woman's enthusiasm.

"Well, Miss Waites, I am happy to say that I think you would suit me very well. You have details of the salary I am offering which I trust you will find to your satisfaction. We set sail on a ship called the *Blue Diamond* which leaves from the port of Southampton.

"If you will leave your address with Cobham, I will see that the tickets and all the information you need are sent round to you this evening."

He rang for the butler to show her out.

Tamina realised she was being dismissed, which was an odd feeling.

She had been quite prepared to continue talking about his work, but she had forgotten for the moment that the Earl only saw her as an employee, not as an equal.

She shook hands with him again, still wondering why there was this air of familiarity about him, then followed the butler along the passage into the impressive hall.

"His Lordship mentioned sending round my travel tickets," she said airily, before remembering that she was not Lady Tamina, but the lowly Tabitha Waites. "I mean, my tickets for the journey – would it be possible to have them sent to Mrs. Shepherd's Agency?"

Cobham looked at her sharply.

She seemed to him a nice well-educated girl and he wondered if perhaps she was from a good family who had fallen on hard times. There was a wealth of breeding and education in her carriage and speech.

He had, for example, noticed her hands when she pulled off her gloves on arriving. Those hands, pale and delicate with perfect oval nails, had never done any hard work in their lives! He was far too aware of people's station in life to be fooled.

"Yes, certainly, Miss Waites. I can arrange that for you."

He did not ask for any reason. He had the feeling that this young lady was in dire need of a job and wondered if she was perhaps living in some very poor area that she did not want the Earl to know about.

Outside in the street Tamina could have jumped for joy.

She had secured the job, she would be escaping from England and leaving Edmund and his treachery behind her.

'I like the Earl, which is a big plus,' she cooed softly to herself as she hurried along the pavement, heading towards a main road where she could find a Hackney cab.

'He seems a fine man, which is important to me. He obviously has a clever mind and his face is kind, although troubled. I would hate to work for someone I could not respect. And I like the idea of his book very much indeed.'

And as dusk was falling, she felt the misery surrounding her since Edmund's betrayal lift a little.

*

If Tamina had glanced behind her just then, she would have seen a fair-haired young man run up the stairs from the basement servants' entrance and hurry off in the other direction.

Joe Goodall was desperate.

All his schemes for eloping with his sweetheart, Nancy, had been thrown into ruin by the Earl's plans to leave England and sail for Madeira.

Obviously the Earl expected Joe to go with him. There was no way he could ask for time off when they were to leave almost immediately.

And as Tamina was being carried across London to Knightsbridge, dreaming of her escape from England, Joe was tapping at a dirty wooden door in a rundown street.

"Nancy! Nancy! Are you there? It's me, Joe."

The door creaked open and a pale scared face peeped out. Then with a terrified glance over her shoulder, the red-headed girl slid out into the street.

"Hush, Joe! Oh, do be quiet. Dad's asleep at the table. But 'e'll be awake any second. He's meetin' some friends down in Picadilly."

Joe drew in his breath in a sharp gasp as the sleeve of Nancy's thin dress fell back to expose a bracelet of black bruises round her wrist.

"The beast! He's done this to you, 'asn't he?"

He went to push past her, but a small hand on his chest stopped him.

"No, Joe! Don't. Oh, please don't. He'll kill you. Don't make me go on livin' without you. I couldn't bear it! *Please.*"

And her large green eyes filled with glistening tears.

Joe forced himself to stand still.

She was right. He knew he was no match for Bill Rider.

The man had been a boxing champion before he grew so fat. He had been known as someone who fought with no mercy and Joe was certain he would show none to anyone who spoke up to him.

"Listen, Nancy. You just 'ave to get away."

"But Joe, 'ow can I? You're off away to foreign parts with the Earl tomorrow! Where can I go? Dad would find me wherever I went and drag me back 'ere. Then he'd take 'is belt to me!"

Joe took her gently by the shoulders and pulled her close.

"Listen, can you be brave, sweetheart?"

He felt her nod.

"Then 'ere's what you must do. Find some boy's clothes, take this guinea and get yourself to the docks at

44

Southampton."

"But Joe – "

"Listen, you can't stay here no longer, Nancy. He'll kill you, sure as eggs is eggs! The only thing you can do is stowaway on the same boat as I'm travellin' on. Ship's Captains can marry people, you know. It's our only chance."

"But Joe – "

Nancy's face was now swept with hope and then resignation.

"No buts, sweetheart. I don't know how long 'is Lordship is thinkin' of stayin' in this Madeira place. He might sail on to somewhere else. He's writin' some old travel book. It could be months and months before I'm back in England. You could be dead by then!

"No, I'll find you at the docks and help you hide somewhere on the boat. Look out for a big ship called the *Blue Diamond*.

"Then when we're a long way out to sea, we'll – we'll – well, somehow I'll find a way for us to marry. I can talk to the Captain. I knows he can marry us. This is our only chance, Nancy, my girl. *You're comin' with me*!"

*

Safely at home once more, Tamina hurried upstairs to her room. She threw off the ghastly green hat she had borrowed from Mrs. Driver the cook and shook her long golden hair free from the myriad of pins she had used to keep it secure.

She sank down at her little writing desk, so pretty with its inlaid patterns of mother-of-pearl.

Tamina stared down at the framed photographs of her beloved family and gained courage from their loving

45

expressions.

Resolutely she pulled paper and ink towards her.

Before she left England, there was one more thing she had to do – and it would be the hardest of all.

She realised that she had never written to Edmund before. He had always insisted that any communication between them should come from him.

But this letter was important for her battered self-esteem.

"Edmund," she wrote, *"I will be brief. This letter is to inform you that I no longer wish to marry you.*

Information has reached me that makes that idea abhorrent to me. I am sure you can guess what it is. From this day there is no longer an engagement between us.

I am leaving London.

Please do not make any attempt to discover my whereabouts or contact me in any way."

And with tears falling like pearls onto the paper, she signed it formally,

"Lady Tamina Braithwaite."

There! She folded the paper and, before she could change her mind, folded it into an envelope.

She would have it delivered to the House of Commons first thing in the morning and then Lady Tamina Braithwaite would disappear and Miss Tabitha Waites would take her place.

CHAPTER FOUR

Three days later, Tamina once again stood waiting in the imposing entrance hall of Daventry House.

It was early in the morning and chilly in the late summer dawn. She was glad of the plain brown cloak she was wearing over her sensible dark fawn travelling suit.

Her long fair hair was twisted up into a severe bun under a very sensible brown felt hat she had bought in a big London store that catered for sensible working ladies.

"The Earl will be with you shortly, Miss Waites," intoned Cobham. "I have arranged for your luggage to be put in the carriage. You will be driving directly to the docks at the port of Southampton."

Tamina nodded. She was too excited to reply.

The last three days had seen a whirlwind of activity. She had collected the tickets from the Agency and smiled at the sum of money the Earl had enclosed. There was enough to buy new wardrobes for several secretaries.

Tamina had placed the five pound notes carefully in her small carved jewellery box.

She had no intention of using the Earl's money to buy clothes. It seemed wrong to be paid anything for this job when she was only doing it to escape from Edmund, not to be a useful working member of society.

She had closed up the family's London house and informed the staff that she was travelling out to Italy to stay with her parents and that she had arranged for them to move down to the family estate in Devon.

Next she had written to her mother, explaining that she was bored with the social scene in London and had agreed to go cruising around the Mediterranean with 'a friend'.

Tamina hated telling even a half truth to her parents, but she knew that if she confessed to what was really happening, her mother would come rushing home and that would cause all sorts of problems for her father in the diplomatic world.

Her biggest problem had been her personal maid, Florence. Obviously, in normal circumstances, she would have taken the young girl to Italy with her.

There was no way she could just leave her behind in England without some explanation.

But just as Tamina was trying to find an excuse to send Florence back to her parents for a holiday – something the young girl would have found astonishing – fate stepped in.

Florence was pouring boiling water into a bowl, the heavy jug slipped in her hand and she suffered a nasty scald on her arm.

Tamina was deeply concerned, but luckily the doctor said that the burn would heal with rest and fresh air.

Florence was sent down to Devon with the rest of the London staff and Tamina could announce that she would employ a maid when she arrived in Italy.

And now her great escape was at last under way.

With her tickets she had also found a note stating

that she should join the Earl for the journey down to Southampton.

"Ah, Miss Waites. It is very pleasing to me to see that you are a believer in punctuality."

The Earl was now running down the great curving staircase towards her, smiling.

"When I find myself waiting for people, I tend to become irritated and that is not a good start to any journey."

Tamina smiled back warmly.

"Indeed, my Lord, I believe it is impolite for anyone to be late for an appointment."

The Earl looked at her keenly.

Slim and pretty, his new secretary's appearance was smart and business-like, except for another hideous hat!

He wondered vaguely why the millinery industry seemed determined to make such ugly apparel for women who could not afford to pay a great deal of money.

But the hat apart, Miss Waites seemed keen and efficient.

How different she seemed to the beautiful Lady Eunice who drifted through life with no aim or goal except to look elegant and was always twenty minutes late for everything!

He had a strong sympathy for working girls such as Miss Waites. She was obviously well educated and her voice was low and melodious and although she was small and slim, she seemed strong.

He wondered if her family had fallen on hard times and decided he would try and discover her story during their time together on the cruise.

"Right, the luggage is in the carriage. Joe!" he

called and his valet appeared. "Let us be away."

Tamina smiled at the servant who nodded his head in greeting. She followed him out to the driveway, wondering why such a young man looked so sad and worried.

'Perhaps he is concerned about going to sea. If he has never travelled, he may think he will be seasick if the ocean becomes rough,' she thought and decided she would try to do all she could to put his mind at rest.

She had travelled by ship several times and was one of the lucky people who had, according to sailors, 'good sea legs'. She never felt ill, even in the roughest of seas.

Her brother, Peter, was a Commander in the Royal Navy and the Braithwaite estate in Devon enjoyed a long seashore. She had sailed in small dinghies with Peter when they were children and felt no fear of the sea.

But Tamina knew that a young man such as Joe, who she imagined had lived in a poorish part of London all his life until he went into service, might never have even seen the ocean and so be terrified of what might happen to him.

However there was no chance to speak to him as Joe clambered up to sit beside the coachman and Tamina realised that she was to sit alone inside the carriage with the Earl.

She was pleased to discover that the Earl was not driving himself as she hoped to learn more about his plans for his book and to find out more about the man himself.

'Can I really trust myself that my opinions about anyone will be correct in the future?' she worried. 'After all, I thought Edmund was the love of my life. I would have vowed on my soul that he was a gentleman of honour and integrity and I was completely wrong!"

Oh, how she hated him! How could love turn to disgust so easily?

Forced to flee the country because of her feelings for a man she knew was not worthy of her.

But she could still feel Edmund's kisses on her mouth and remember the ecstasy she had experienced when he held her in his arms.

How could he have been so deceitful, not just to her, but to that other poor girl who believed they were already engaged and that he was intending for *them* to share a life together?

But as the carriage left London and headed down the busy roads towards Southampton, Tamina realised that she must stop tormenting herself over the past.

'What I must do,' she lectured herself, 'is to leave behind everything that has happened in London and start a different life for better or worse. I must start anew and think anew. But I am certain that in a great many ways it is not going to be easy.'

"I shall be glad to be away from England," the Earl murmured, almost to himself and Tamina started. His words echoed her thoughts exactly.

He must have noticed her surprised expression because he hastily added,

"Oh, do not misunderstand me, Miss Waites! I love my country passionately and even though I have lived abroad a great deal, I always knew that this was home and where I would spend the rest of my life. But I have – reasons – to be happy to be away at the moment."

Tamina glanced at his dark brooding expression and she could see that as hard as he tried to hide it, the Earl had been deeply hurt recently.

And she sensed that this was more than just the normal grief to be expected on the death of his older brother. She understood because she was in the same emotional state that this was very personal.

She opened her mouth to ask a gentle question and then stopped.

Of course she could not do anything of the sort! She was only Tabitha Waites, the secretary, not Lady Tamina Braithwaite, his social equal.

She must not forget her new position in life for an instant!

"So, Miss Waites," enquired the Earl, pulling his thoughts away from Lady Eunice and her betrayal, "are you looking forward to our expedition?"

"Certainly," replied Tamina, her blue eyes bright with excitement. "I love travel, my Lord, and I am especially interested in your book. Will you please explain a little more about your ideas."

The Earl smiled at her, the tight bands of despair easing a little around his chest.

Wisps of golden hair had escaped from under the hideous brown hat and curled on her pink cheeks.

Miss Waites made a very attractive companion.

"It will be a mixture of history and new travel information. Madeira is to be our first stop and so I will be starting the book with a chapter about that island."

"Madeira sounds wonderful!"

"Yes, it is a fascinating place. An old volcano rising up out of the sea and becoming a magical island with an incredible landscape. One side of the island is all rocks and steep cliffs, but the other is full of flowers and lemon and orange trees. It is truly enchanting.

"But my book must not be just a dry list of facts and figures. I am a great believer that when you feel strongly about a place, you should let it show."

"And have you been working on this idea for some time, my Lord?"

"I started this book some months before I arrived in England, but I threw that manuscript away because I was annoyed with what I had written. There seemed nothing different from what has been published many times before."

The Earl's dark eyes gleamed with enthusiasm.

"This attempt will contain more passion, more feeling."

His expression changed.

"Unfortunately, I do have so much more personal experience to bring to my work now."

Tamina nodded and then to her horror she felt tears forming in her eyes.

"I think books should always stir your emotions," she whispered. "I feel honoured to help you produce such a work."

The Earl reached forward suddenly, as if he was about to touch her gloved hand before sitting back again, as if he had forgotten for a moment that he was speaking to a member of his staff.

"You are indeed very young to feel so deeply," he commented cautiously. "Do you have trouble in your life? If there is anything I can do to help – "

Tamina shook her head.

This was dangerous ground. She must never let her guard slip again.

If the Earl ever discovered who she really was, he

would never trust her again and would probably send her straight home.

"That is most kind of you, my Lord, but I can assure you there is no trouble in my life at all."

The rest of the journey passed swiftly and soon Tamina was feeling a thrill of excitement when the vast bulk of the cruise liner, the *Blue Diamond*, came into view.

Tall white sides studded with endless portholes towered above her head. Crowds of excited people were rushing up and down the gangways – telegraph boys, florists, porters with carts of luggage.

Flocks of seagulls soared through the air crying raucously and circling the two funnels with their bright blue diamond patterns whilst the breeze blowing off the Solent was salty and invigorating.

"Joe? Joe? Where on earth has the boy got to?"

The Earl had jumped out of the carriage and was staring round for his valet who had disappeared into the crowd.

Tamina had been waiting automatically on the top step to be handed out of the carriage, but bit back a little smile as she realised that was not going to happen. She was a working girl, not a lady, in the Earl's eyes.

But she was wrong.

As she started to step down, the Earl spun round and his strong hand slid under her arm to help her.

"Thank you, my Lord," she murmured.

"I think Joe must have gone ahead to search for my main luggage," remarked the Earl. "It was sent down to the ship earlier."

He sighed.

"He should have waited until I told him to leave, but

Joe is very young and not quite sure yet exactly what his duties are."

"But he seems a steady young man, my Lord."

"Indeed. He is, I believe, very much like his brother, Jacob."

The Earl sighed again heavily and his dark eyes grew even darker.

"He – Jacob, was with my brother when the accident happened. He never left his side although he was mortally injured himself. He even managed to write down my brother's last words for me before he passed away. I owe Joe's family a great debt."

Tamina nodded, but inwardly she was frowning.

As she had stood for those few seconds on the top step of the carriage, she had been able to look out over the heads of the crowd.

She had seen Joe in deep discussion with one of the young telegraph boys. And she had seen Joe and the boy wearing a dark green uniform, hurrying up the far gangway.

'It seems he has accidentally met a friend from London,' she thought, 'but he should not have abandoned his Lordship in such a manner.'

As they both reached the bottom of the first class gangway, Tamina braced herself to part from the Earl.

She was well aware that as his secretary, she would have a cabin in the second class tier of the ship.

The Earl stopped and gestured to her to precede him.

"I have just changed the cabin allocation," he said briefly at her look of astonishment. "I never know when I will want to work on my book. Sometimes it can be late at night and I will not wish to kick my heels until you are summoned from a lower deck, Miss Waites."

"Yes, of course, my Lord. It will be very pleasant to be in the first class section and, as you say, it will make our working together far easier."

"So you have no problems with working late at night?" asked the Earl as they climbed the steep gangway under the flapping white awning that protected them from the salty breeze.

"None at all, my Lord. When I undertake a job, I do not feel I should only work between certain hours. I am more than ready to help whenever you wish."

They had reached the top of the gangway and the Earl nodded his head, his dark eyes warm with approval.

He was struck again by Miss Waites's sincerity and hardworking approach to life. He was certain she would never betray any trust laid upon her slim shoulders.

Just then, a young ship's Officer stepped forward to greet them. Tall and good-looking, he had bright grey eyes in a tanned face and under his cap Tamina could see hair that was as blond as her own.

"My Lord, my name is Lieutenant Archie Oxburn. On behalf of Captain Reid and the Shipping Company, may I welcome you on board and wish you a pleasant trip."

"Thank you, Lieutenant. This is my secretary, Miss Waites. I believe my valet is attending to our luggage."

The young Officer held out his hand to Tamina.

"Good morning, Miss Waites. Welcome aboard the *Blue Diamond*. I trust you will find everything to your liking."

"I am sure I shall, Lieutenant Oxburn. She seems a marvellous ship."

The tall young Officer laughed down at her.

"Oh, I see you are well aware that ships are always referred to as feminine?"

Tamina smiled.

"Indeed, yes. I have an older brother – "

She stopped abruptly and then realising that she had to continue, took a deep breath and added,

"Yes, I have a brother in the Navy. He has told me so many times."

"A brother in the Navy? Which ship is he serving in? Our paths may have crossed."

"I fear we are blocking the gangway," interrupted the Earl before Tamina could reply.

The Lieutenant frowned apologetically and at once signalled to a Steward to escort them to their cabins.

But just as Tamina was about to take her leave, she turned and saw Joe at the far end of the companionway, still talking to the young boy in the dark green uniform.

Her heart sank.

She was sure the Earl was not the type of gentleman to censure one of his staff out of hand, but there was no denying the fact that the young man was not behaving well.

It would be dreadful to have a bad and unhappy atmosphere right at the beginning of the trip.

Swiftly she turned back towards Lieutenant Oxburn, blocking the valet from the Earl's view and raising her voice slightly to say,

"Oh, I am so looking forward to leaving harbour. Will there be a band playing?"

The Lieutenant looked surprised before replying

warmly,

"Indeed there will be. Streamers are thrown from the railings on the Promenade Deck and all the well-wishers who have gathered to wish us *bon voyage* wave and throw streamers back. I shall be delighted to escort you – if your Lordship agrees?"

"Oh, no, that won't be necessary – I only – "

"Certainly, Miss Waites," the Early broke in, his face now stern and distant, unlike his earlier friendly countenance. "I would not wish to stand in your way of enjoying the ceremony. I have experienced a ship leaving port many times."

Tamina murmured her thanks, but as she followed the Steward along corridors and up staircases towards her cabin, she felt strangely irritated and ill at ease.

She had no desire to watch the leaving ceremony with Lieutenant Archie Oxburn at her side and even to her eyes she knew she had appeared forward.

But the damage had been done, but maybe this was exactly how a Tabitha Waites would act on board her first voyage.

At least the Earl had not noticed Joe ushering his young friend away.

*

In all the hustle and bustle of a big cruise liner getting ready to sail, no one paid any attention to the two young men as they hurried along the deck.

Joe glanced down at Nancy – he had been quite astonished when he had realised that the green-uniformed youth waving to him as the carriage drove into the docks was the girl he loved so much.

"Where did you get the uniform?" he hissed,

glancing over his shoulder to where the Earl and the new secretary were climbing out of the carriage.

"It's Charlie's, he lives next door but one," Nancy told him softly. "He broke 'is leg last week and can't work. I gave 'im a shillin' to borrow it!"

Joe squeezed her arm and hurried her up the gangway.

With her beautiful red hair pushed up under her hat, she passed for a young boy, as long as no one looked too closely.

And there were several messenger boys running back and forward from the harbour offices to the ship. No one was going to notice one in particular.

"I must get you stowed away somewhere safe," urged Joe.

Nancy was shaking, she was so scared.

Running away from home and escaping from her tyrannical and brutal father was a huge step to take, but stowing away on this ship with Joe was an even bigger one.

"Oh Joe, are we doin' the right thing?" she growned. "There's still time for me to go 'ome. I can tell Dad I had to go to t'other side of London to buy 'im a nice piece of fish."

"He wouldn't believe you, sweetheart. He'd take his belt to you again!"

"But Joe, what if this Captain won't marry us? What if your Master finds out and dismisses you?"

"Then I'll think of some other plan, but you're not goin' back to that devil, Nancy! You're my girl and you're stayin' with me."

At the end of the long first class corridor, Joe found

a small metal doorway standing ajar. He pushed it open and discovered an iron ladder leading down through a maze of pipes.

At the bottom where the ladder turned in the other direction and vanished through a hatch to another deck, there was a sheltered area behind a stack of boxes.

"Here!" Joe said glancing round. "Stay 'ere for now. I'll bring you food and blankets as soon as we sail."

"But Joe – what about – you know – I'll need the bathroom!" Nancy whispered, her face going red.

Joe cursed under his breath.

"Don't worry. I noticed one just along that top corridor. It'll be the one us servants who are cabined in first class 'ave to use. I'll get you in and out when the coast is clear."

He gave her a quick kiss, then clambered up the ladder and raced along to the Earl's cabin, grabbing an armful of clean towels off a trolley as he passed.

"Joe! I've been calling for you," snapped the Earl impatiently as he knocked and entered the big cabin.

"Sorry, my Lord. I've been obtainin' some extra towels. I didn't think the bathroom had been stocked adequately for your needs."

The Earl shot him a sharp look.

The boy looked jumpy and nervous. He wondered if he was worried about going to sea and decided to keep him busy so he would not have time to think about feeling ill.

Suddenly there came the booming roar of the ship's siren.

They were about to sail and through the open porthole of his elegant cabin, he could hear the cheering crowds and the blare of the brass band playing on deck.

The Earl turned away to his desk and began to sort out the reference books he had brought with him. He wondered if Miss Waites was on deck, watching the fun.

Well, there was no reason why she should miss it. Just because that ship's Officer had seemed such a callow youth, peacocking around in his white uniform.

He slammed a book shut, making Joe, who was unpacking one of his trunks, jump and drop an armful of dress shirts.

Just then there was a quiet knock on the cabin door.

Joe answered it and announced that Miss Waites would like to speak to the Earl if it was convenient.

"Come in!" called the Earl, greeting her eagerly and suppressing a wry smile that she was still wearing that ridiculous brown hat.

"I hope your cabin is satisfactory? Is there a problem? I had imagined you to be on deck waving goodbye to England."

Tamina shook her head gravely.

"No problem at all, my Lord. My cabin is very charming and I would like to thank you for arranging for me to be on this deck. And I am afraid that loud ceremonies such as those going on at present hold no interest for me. I was just trying to be polite to the young Officer.

"No, I have come to see you because so far I have done nothing to earn my wages! I was wondering if there was anything you needed me to do for you right away. Perhaps letters or telegrams you would like me to write out."

The black mood that had for some reason settled on

the Earl's broad shoulders slipped away.

The room seemed more comfortable, the air lighter and he could even enjoy the cheering and the music playing on deck.

"No, Miss Waites, I think tomorrow morning will be a good time to start our work. For the rest of the day I suggest you explore the ship. It seems a very fine vessel."

Tamina murmured her thanks and left the room.

She returned to her cabin feeling suddenly a little lonely. How nice it would have been if the Earl had suggested accompanying her on a journey of discovery.

But, of course, he could not.

Tonight he would eat his dinner in the first class dining room and she would find a seat in the second class area, no doubt being escorted to a table where other single ladies were seated.

She pulled off her horrible hat and began to brush out her long golden hair, wondering why she was not feeling happy.

She was about to embark on a marvellous adventure and she was escaping from England and Edmund.

There was no reason at all to feel miserable she chided herself.

But she did.

CHAPTER FIVE

Tamina had just returned to her cabin after a brisk walk along the Promenade Deck. The sun was setting and the greeny-grey waters of the English Channel were touched with gold and crimson as it dipped into the Western sky.

The walk had cheered her immensely.

She had felt a rush of freedom once England had disappeared into the distance and she could no longer see land.

Edmund and all her worries were already beginning to fade and she realised that perhaps her heart had not been broken as thoroughly as she had originally thought.

Tamina had washed and changed for dinner, hoping that her blue skirt and white lawn blouse with a single strand of pearls would be considered the right attire for a working girl.

She was just folding her hair into a severe French pleat, suitable for a secretary, when a tap at the door heralded Joe.

"A message from 'is Lordship, Miss Waites," he said. "He asks if you would dine with 'im this evenin' as he wishes to discuss a work plan for 'is book."

Tamina felt her cheeks glow pink and she turned

away so the young valet could not see how pleased she was.

Of course it was just a working meal with her employer, but she was still delighted to be invited.

The first class restaurant was a blaze of light and noise as Tamina walked through the door.

A trio of musicians were playing pleasant music, a background to the murmur of voices and the tinkle of knives and forks as the meal was served.

Great ornate pillars of blue marble divided the room into comfortable sections and the vast glass chandeliers gleamed down onto the vivid colours of the ladies' dresses and the austere black and white of the gentlemen in their dinner jackets.

It was a magnificent room.

The linen tablecloths and napkins were pure snowy white and the glasses and cutlery gleamed in the brilliant light, sending sparks of colour around the room.

On each table was a bowl full of blue and white flowers – the Diamond Shipping Company colours.

The same blue could be found on the china menu holders and napkin rings and the seats of the gilt chairs were covered in dark blue velvet.

The weather since they set sail had been so calm and peaceful that only a few of the passengers had succumbed to seasickness and most of the tables were full.

"Lord Daventry's table, please," she murmured to the Head-waiter and was immediately escorted through the throng of diners to the best part of the room, well away from the serving doors and the musicians.

The Earl, immaculate in white tie and tails, stood as she approached and she smiled as the waiter held a gilt chair for her.

"Thank you so much for asking me to dine, my Lord. I am grateful for a chance to see this lovely room."

The Earl smiled and beckoned to a waiter to pour the wine.

He was conscious that explanations about his book could easily have waited until the next morning, but he had not wanted to eat alone.

No, he had wanted to observe the expression in Miss Waites's startling sapphire eyes as she gazed round, taking in the scene.

Even dressed simply and soberly, she shone like a blazing candle flame. Her fine white blouse and simple pearl necklet made the evening gowns of the other women look loud and tawdry, no matter how many diamonds and rubies they were wearing.

"Did you bring a ball gown with you, Miss Waites?" he asked suddenly as they sipped a superb consommé enriched with dry sherry to give it extra flavour.

Tamina glanced across the white roses and blue cornflowers of the table centre-piece.

"Why yes, I did, my Lord. I was not sure if you would require me to attend any formal functions to take notes. I would have changed tonight, but Joe led me to believe you were already waiting to dine and I already know your views well about ladies being late for their appointments!"

The Earl smiled.

"The Captain will be holding a select party tomorrow night, followed by dinner and dancing. I would suggest you dress formally and attend with me as there might well be comments I need you to write down as I think of them."

Tamina felt her cheeks flush.

"I brought a notebook and pencil with me tonight for just such a purpose," she said, indicating her leather bag, not wanting him to think she had considered this anything other than a business meeting.

The Earl pushed his soup bowl to one side.

He was sure there were all sorts of points about the history of Madeira and interesting places to see on the island that he should be committing to paper, but at the moment he could think of none of them.

His gaze fell once again on the smooth creamy skin of her neck where the pearl necklet gleamed.

He frowned – if he was not mistaken, that was a very fine piece of jewellery.

He wondered how a mere secretary came to own such an expensive item. A present from an ex-employer, perhaps? But why should anyone buy a young woman such a valuable piece?

"Your necklet – " he began suspiciously.

Tamina raised a hand to finger the pearls, her eyes lighting with happiness.

"A gift from my brothers," she responded warmly. "For my sixteenth birthday. I love it because it is so beautiful, but I love it even more because they chose it for me."

The Earl's frown vanished.

How stupid of him. Of course any jewellery a young girl like Miss Waites owned could only be gifts from her immediate family.

She was not another Lady Eunice.

There was certainly no dissembling in *her* nature, no subterfuge or lies. No betrayal of her honour.

'And even if it had been a present from another man, why should that worry me?' he thought angrily. 'Tabitha Waites is just my secretary. A hard working girl I employ to do a job.'

And he decided that he would refrain from asking her any more questions about her life.

The rest of the meal passed swiftly. A beautifully cooked lemon sole followed by a lightly spiced roasted chicken.

But by the time the fresh fruit was served, Tamina felt that some of the sparkle had died out of the evening, although she could not understand why.

She was aware of many people watching her as the Earl escorted her out of the dining room.

She felt her lips twitch as she fought back a smile.

How awkward it would be if any of those present recognised her! She had seen no familiar faces, but life has a strange way of producing odd coincidences.

"Would you care to take a turn on the deck before retiring?" the Earl suggested.

Tamina nodded.

"That would be very agreeable. I love to look at the moon reflected on the sea. It is so beautiful."

"Do you need a coat, Miss Waites?"

Tamina shook her head, unaware that a lock of golden hair had escaped her chignon and was lying across her shoulder.

"No, thank you, my Lord. My wrap is made of velvet and quite warm. And there is no breeze tonight."

Together they walked along the Promenade deck amongst several other passengers who were taking the night air. But the further they walked, the crowds thinned until at last they were the only couple on that part of the deck.

Tamina now stopped and leaning against the railing gazed out in awe to where the moon was rising, casting a ribbon of silver across the dark sea.

"Oh, how wonderful!" she exclaimed.

The Earl stared down at her face.

He had an absurd desire to reach out and tuck back behind her ear the stray blonde curl that had escaped its bonds.

He cursed silently under his breath. What was wrong with him? This was moon madness.

"Well, we have a busy day ahead of us," he said formally. "We had better retire."

Then he felt a wave of irritation against himself because the young girl's wondering expression was wiped away and again there was the self-possessed secretary once more.

The Earl escorted Tamina back to her cabin and bade her a brief goodnight.

She watched as he walked away along the corridor to his stateroom, puzzled as to why his relaxed demeanour in the early part of the evening had changed so drastically.

Had it been her fault? Did he find her company boring?

She knew she had a tendency to chatter – her old Nanny had always told her that she talked too much.

Some gentlemen did not like that, especially at meal times. Tamina resolved to be a little more reserved if the occasion arose again.

She did not sleep well that night.

She told herself it was because of the strange bed, the rocking of the ship and that she was still heartsick by Edmund and his betrayal.

But she knew that it was none of them that stood between her and slumber. It was the look in a pair of dark brown eyes that she could see as soon as she closed her own and tried to sleep.

*

The next morning there was a distinct swell and the sky outside Tamina's porthole looked sullen, grey and overcast.

She dressed swiftly, determined to be ready for whatever the day held in store.

Her face looked pale in the dressing table mirror and she was angry with herself for getting so little rest.

The Earl of Daventry was indeed an interesting and fascinating man, there was no doubt about it. He was also her employer! That was the fact that she must not forget, she told herself firmly.

Lying awake wondering what his opinion of her might be was a completely useless exercise.

As she walked out of her room into the passage she stopped.

A few yards ahead of her she could see Joe.

She was just about to call out a cheerful "good morning," but she hesitated.

The young man was carrying a bundle wrapped in a napkin. He was hurrying along the passageway, glancing uneasily from side to side, almost as if he was scared someone would catch him.

Two elderly passengers now appeared from their staterooms. They nodded a brief good morning to her and Tamina smiled in return, but kept them between her and Joe.

She was not quite sure why she wanted to know what he was doing.

He could be on an errand for the Earl, of course, but somehow she did not think he was.

She turned a corner cautiously and then stopped.

The passageway stretched in front of her. There were now several people making their way towards the stairway, but there was no sign of Joe!

Tamina frowned.

Where could he have gone? There was no door to the outer deck along this part of the companionway. He must have entered another cabin.

Gravely she made her way towards the second class dining room for breakfast. She was seated at a table with two other single ladies who were travelling on their own.

But Tamina found it now difficult to make polite conversation.

Yes, the ship was wonderful and no, she did not feel the slightest bit seasick. Yes, she was working for the Earl of Daventry and yes, the tragedy that had befallen his family was terrible and yes, he was a kind and considerate employer.

But as she chatted politely, sipped her coffee, nibbled on a piece of toast and wondered –

Joe's whole demeanour had seemed so suspicious. And what had he been carrying so secretly inside that napkin?

Tamina knew why she was worried.

'The Earl has endured so much tragedy and loss recently,' she said to herself. 'He sets such store on loyalty that I feel he would be devastated if he discovered Joe was a thief or some kind of criminal.'

After breakfast Tamina took a short brisk walk along an outside deck enjoying the steady breeze that brought colour into her cheeks.

She did not find the increasingly rough motion of the ship unpleasant, although she could tell by the pale green faces of some of her companions that they were suffering from the onset of seasickness!

At ten o'clock precisely, she tapped on the door of the Earl's stateroom.

Joe led her through to a large sitting room where the Earl was seated at his desk. He was wearing a green brocade waistcoat, but his jacket was thrown across the back of his chair and with his shirt sleeves rolled up, he looked much younger and less stern this morning.

He was freshly shaved, but his thick dark hair was tousled, as if the brush had given up the fight!

The desk was covered with books and papers and he waved his hand at them as he greeted Tamina.

"Ah, good morning, Miss Waites. I trust you slept well?"

"Very well, thank you, my Lord."

"And you are ready to begin work?"

Tamina drew out a large notepad from the leather holdall she was carrying.

"Yes, indeed. I am only surprised, my Lord, to see that you have already begun."

The Earl smiled and ran slim fingers through his

hair, making it clear to Tamina exactly why it was so untidy this early in the morning.

"I wanted to put my notes and thoughts in order before you arrived, Miss Waites. I have been told by one of the crew that the weather may well deteriorate this evening and so there is every chance that we will be unable to work tomorrow."

Tamina settled herself in a chair at the other side of the desk and looked at him, trying not to smile.

"Do you suffer from *mal-de-mer*, my Lord?"

He looked up, startled.

"What? No, I certainly do not, but I had wondered if you – "

Tamina shook her head.

"I am an extremely good sailor, my Lord. I shall report for work at ten o'clock regardless of the weather conditions."

The Earl's dark eyes gleamed.

"I hear the sound of a challenge in your words, Miss Waites. Are we to see which of us succumbs first?"

Tamina doodled a neat row of circles on her writing pad and then glanced up at her employer, her blue eyes brilliant under thick lashes.

"I have the strongest feeling that you think because I am a woman, I will automatically become seasick!"

He leant back in his chair, a grin flickering across his well-shaped mouth.

"I would never presume to think that of you, Miss Waites! But you must allow me the fact that the female of the species is not as strong as the male."

Tamina chuckled.

"I believe that seasickness is not an affliction that discriminates between men and women, my Lord."

He laughed.

"Well, we will no doubt see tonight. I suggest we both keep our fingers well crossed. Now, let us get to work. I will dictate a few notes about Madeira and then we can work on each one individually."

The morning flashed past.

At some point Joe came in with a tray of coffee and biscuits, but the work continued.

Tamina could not remember the last time when she had enjoyed herself so much. The Earl's notes for his book were varied and interesting.

He was quite obviously extremely well educated, but there was a descriptive quality to his words as he talked about the countryside that intrigued Tamina, because it showed a sensitive side to his nature that she was sure he would always do his best to hide.

It was past one o'clock when Tamina unconsciously sighed as the Earl paused while dictating. She stretched her fingers which were feeling stiff and cramped from holding the pencil for so long.

The Earl glanced up, pulling his mind back from the history of Madeira to the present day.

"Miss Waites, my apologies!" He glanced at his watch. "I had no idea it was so late. Why didn't you speak up? You must be hungry."

Tamina wriggled her aching shoulders.

"It has all been so interesting, my Lord, that I did not realise the time either. But I must admit that now you have mentioned it, luncheon does seem a pleasant prospect!"

"Yes, luncheon." There was a pause before he continued, "do not let me keep you a moment longer. I will see you back here at three o'clock."

Tamina stood and hesitated.

For a long second she had thought that he might ask her to eat with him and when he did not speak, she felt silly and stupid.

She turned swiftly and so did not see him look up, the words forming an invitation on his lips.

Outside in the companionway, a hot and flustered Tamina decided to head back to her cabin to tidy herself before facing the second class dining room again.

She bathed her face with cool water, trying to calm the turmoil that raged within her.

Why had she ever imagined that the Earl would want to ask her to lunch with him? Last night had been a mere courtesy to a young employee. Today they were back in their strict roles and she would do very well to remember it.

But a little voice in her head murmured that she wished, oh, how she wished, that she was Lady Tamina Braithwaite on board this ship and not plain Miss Tabitha Waites.

Dabbing a little lavender water behind her ears, she tightened the pins holding up her long hair and left the cabin.

Just as she turned the corner of her companionway to head for the stairs, she stopped.

There! It was young Joe again! Hurrying along head down, clutching another bundle wrapped in a linen napkin, he looked the very picture of a suspicious character.

Then, to Tamina's astonishment, he stopped and tried to open what looked like a heavy metal door leading to one of the 'out of bounds' areas of the ship.

But the door must have become jammed in some way, because he had to put down his bundle and use both hands to pull it open.

And as he did so, two bread rolls and a piece of cheese rolled out onto the floor.

Tamina took an impulsive step forward, but stopped. In the corridor behind her, a door had opened and she could hear voices.

She recognised one of them. It was the young ship's Officer she had met yesterday, Lieutenant Archie Oxburn.

Oh, this was dreadful! If he spotted Joe trying to access a forbidden area of the ship for whatever reason, he would surely have to report him to the Earl.

There would be all sorts of trouble and distress for everyone and Tamina recognised that the Earl would feel extremely let down if Joe proved to be dishonest, even if it was just food he was stealing.

She spun on her heel, paused and then just as the Lieutenant came round the corner, she almost threw herself forward, as if she had been running.

Inevitably they collided and he put out his arms to catch Tamina as she staggered and nearly fell.

"Goodness! Be careful! Why, Miss Waites, it is you. Are you all right? I haven't hurt you, I trust. Where were you off to in such a hurry? You must be careful of these sharp bends. It is an awkward part of the deck layout just here."

Tamina laughed nervously and clutched at his arms, pretending to sway.

She could see that the Officer's attention was all on her and could only pray that Joe had managed to pull the door open and had vanished about his business – whatever it was.

"I thought I had my sea legs, Lieutenant, but perhaps I was being too optimistic!"

"It does take a little while," he replied, his blue eyes twinkling. "And there is a forecast for bad weather tonight, so do take great care if you are on deck."

"I will. Thank you so much for your concern."

"Are you enjoying the voyage so far?"

"Yes, indeed I am. The *Blue Diamond* is a really beautiful ship."

He nodded enthusiastically, apparently unaware that he was still holding Tamina to stop her falling.

"Yes, the *Blue Diamond* is the largest vessel the Diamond Company has ever built and a very fine liner. But of course she is small in comparison to others that sail the Atlantic.

"Indeed, I wonder if you have heard of the great ship the White Star Line is building! A luxury liner that will be unsinkable, the great *Titanic*!"

"I have heard of it. My – " she hesitated.

She had been going to say 'my Papa has often talked about it' when she realised that might open up all sorts of avenues of conversation about her life as Tabitha Waites.

She went on,

"My desire has been to one day travel aboard such a vessel, but in the meantime this ship is marvellous enough for me. Oh! – "

She broke away from the Lieutenant as the Earl

came round the corner and, with a face like thunder, eased past them with an abrupt nod of his head and a curt "excuse me!"

Tamina felt the blood drain from her face and tears prick her eyes.

What would the Earl be thinking?

That she was flirting with Archie Oxburn?

And what was worse was that there was no way she could possibly ever explain to him how she came to be in such a position.

Muttering a low flustered apology to the Lieutenant, saying she had to meet someone for luncheon, Tamina fled along the corridor and down the stairway towards the dining room.

Appetising smells were wafting out and inside all was cheerful hustle and bustle.

But Tamina hesitated.

Eating was the last thing she wanted to do and if she had to make conversation with another single lady, she would scream.

All she wanted was to explain the situation to the Earl, but of course she could not and why should she think he would be interested anyway.

A ship's Officer was quite a respectable attachment for a secretary. The Earl probably thought she was a flirt, who had seen a good chance of making a match.

'But why am I feeling *so* upset?' she asked herself. 'Goodness, I didn't feel this unhappy when I discovered Edmund's betrayal!'

Trying to quell the emotion that flooded through her veins, she made her way back to the corridor where she had last seen Joe.

It was quiet and empty. Everyone was at luncheon or lying down, trying to cope with the swell that was growing stronger with every passing second.

The hatchway that Joe had struggled to open was shut now, but Tamina could see that the door was not completely closed.

The latch had half caught and it only took a hard pull to open it again.

A waft of cold air blew against her face as she hesitantly stepped inside the compartment. At her feet a steep iron ladder led down into a dark well.

The noise of the great engines sounded louder here, magnified by the metal surroundings.

Now the ship was beginning to rock more violently and Tamina clung to the ladder.

Suddenly she heard a moan.

"Who's there?" she called nervously.

She thought she heard a grunt and then nothing.

"Come out, whoever you are!" she called and when no one replied, she swung herself off the platform and started down the ladder.

As she felt for each rung with her feet, a swift thought flashed through her mind. All those years of playing with her brothers, climbing trees, swinging on ropes and being a madcap tomboy were now paying off.

She had no fear of heights and the ladder was a simple exercise to someone whose brothers had once suspended her on a rope over the edge of a quarry to see how long it would take her to climb up it!

At the bottom of the ladder she turned.

It was dark but a little light was seeping in from another hatchway on a deck below.

Tamina stepped forward and then stopped, gasping, as a cry broke out and her foot touched something – or someone!

CHAPTER SIX

Tamina gulped as her foot touched a body lying on the small metal platform that formed a junction between two ladders vanishing down into the dark depths of the great ship.

She staggered as the ship rolled again. The seas were getting much rougher and it was harder to keep her balance.

"What? Who – Joe is that you?"

Another grunt and then young Joe appeared from the shadows looking white and worried.

"Joe! There you are – but then who is – Oh! – "

As Tamina stared down at the deck, her eyes became more and more used to the dim light.

She could see that what she had thought to be a heap of rags was in fact a young woman, lying wrapped in a dark blue travelling rug that boldly showed the golden insignia of the Earl of Daventry in one corner.

Beneath it she appeared to be dressed in male costume of some dark green colour, but in the poor light it was hard to be sure.

The girl's face was very pale and even her lips were white.

She had long bright red hair that was spilling across the rug down onto the cold metal deck. She was moaning gently and was obviously very unwell.

"Joe? What is happening? Who is this girl? Why are you hiding her down here?"

Joe turned anguished eyes in her direction.

"Oh, Miss Waites, *please* don't tell the Earl! We're not doin' any 'arm, but Nancy 'ere has been so sick with the movement of the boat. I can't get 'er to eat or drink anythin'."

Tamina knelt beside the girl and stroked her pale forehead, which felt damp and hot under her hand.

She looked up, her beautiful face serious.

"But Joe, who is she?"

"My betrothed, miss. Her name's Nancy Rider. We was runnin' away to Gretna Green to get wed, then the Earl announced he was goin' on this boat for a long time and I was to go with 'im. So I 'ad to bring Nancy with me."

Tamina struggled to understand the story.

"Why were you eloping?"

"On account of 'er rotten old father, miss. He beats 'er somethin' brutal, so he does, and I'm not havin' it any longer. I reckoned if we was wed, then he couldn't touch 'er again. She'd belong to me."

Tamina stood up, her blue eyes filled with concern.

"But Joe, Nancy cannot possibly stay down here! She's obviously very seasick and has a fever. She should be helped to a bed and given some care. You must let me tell the Earl at once."

Swiftly Joe reached out and grabbed her arm.

"*No*, miss! You mustn't be doin' that! I'll lose my position and then be turned out onto the street without a reference. And if I don't 'ave a job, I can't marry Nancy.

"She's just feelin' the motion of this boat badly, that's all. She's never been to sea before. Well, nor 'ave I, but I reckon it's a bit like ridin' on the back of the big coach when the 'orses move it along fast. I can cope easily. When it's calm, I'm sure she'll be all right."

Tamina stared at him before reaching out to catch hold of a railing as the ship rolled suddenly before righting itself again.

She was aware that the movement was becoming more and more violent each minute and, as she stared down over the thin iron rail into the darkness below, the little metal platform did not seem that secure a haven for a sick girl.

"I am sorry, Joe, but you must trust the Earl to do the right thing by you. Whatever happens, Nancy cannot stay down here in the cold and dark! And she is alone all while you are serving your Master. That is appalling. I *cannot* allow this to continue."

Joe scowled.

"But it ain't up to you to poke your nose in, is it, miss? Why does it matter to you what we do? Do you want to see us both arrested and thrown into prison or turned out into the street without a name or a penny to save us?"

Tamina began to retort, but hesitated, realising that she was thinking and acting just like Lady Tamina Braithwaite, not plain Miss Tabitha Waites.

And, of course, what Joe did not know was that she too was on board the ship under false pretences.

How could she be such a hypocrite as to report this silly young couple to the authorities when she was doing something just as reprehensible? When, in fact, she had kept her own engagement to Edmund hidden away from her friends and family.

Another consideration was how the Earl would feel when he knew that the young man he had trusted, had promoted to a senior position in his household and had not felt able to confide in him in such a delicate matter.

Now Tamina knew the Earl better and had listened to the words and ideas he wanted to include in his book, she was convinced that beneath the stern exterior was a man of great sensitivity and kindness.

She was certain that he would be deeply upset and troubled by what he would see as Joe's duplicity. And she found herself desperately wanting to save her employer from the pain of those feelings.

Why she should be so determined to help him was something she realised she would have to think about later when she had a quiet moment to sort out her feelings and emotions.

"Joe, truly I do not want to get you and Nancy into trouble. I'll say nothing to the Earl, I promise, but on one condition, that this evening you bring Nancy to my cabin. She can stay there just until we reach Madeira and then somehow you must arrange for her to go ashore."

The ship rolled again and Joe staggered against the ladder.

"But what would she do in a foreign country, miss, without me to look out for her? She don't 'ave any words of a foreign language. A young girl could easily fall prey to all sorts of villains."

Tamina sighed.

It would have been so easy to have given Joe enough money to buy the girl a ticket on a ship heading for England, but the funds of a Miss Waites would not be the same as those of Lady Tamina.

Joe would have known immediately something was wrong if she had offered him such a sum.

"There is, I believe, a large English community living in Funchal, the capital of Madeira, where we dock," she said slowly.

"I am sure there will be employment available for Nancy, perhaps as a lady's maid or children's nurse. The gentry there often travel back to England so I am sure she will be able to go home within a few months and by then you too may be back from your travels with his Lordship."

Tamina fell silent, watching Joe's anxious face as he tried to decide what to do.

She staggered again as the ship pitched violently and blessed the fact that so far she did not seem to be bothered by *mal de mer*.

"*Joe –* "

A weak voice from the deck made them both glance down.

Nancy was awake, tears in her eyes, her face and lips as white as snow.

"Joe – I think the lady's right. I can't stay 'ere no more. I'm so cold, Joe. So very cold. But hot as well!"

The young valet sighed and then rubbed his fingers through his fair hair as if he wanted to scrub his troubles away.

"All right, miss. I'll bring Nancy up to your cabin tonight, when everyone's at dinner and out of the way."

Tamina hesitated and then nodded,

There was nothing else she could do except pat Nancy's hand and tell her to be brave for just a little while longer.

She climbed back up the ladder and through the heavy metal door into the passageway.

A quick glance at her watch told her that she had missed the chance of luncheon and the Earl would be waiting for her in his stateroom.

She just had time to hurry back to her cabin, wash off the grime and oil from her hands and change her blouse which was covered with dirt from the ladder.

Tamina stared at her anxious expression in the mirror as the ship heaved and rolled ominously.

The sea was much rougher and they were obviously in for a violent storm.

She peered out of the porthole, but it was spattered with foam and she could see nothing except for a glimpse of the dark grey ocean covered in curling waves and drifting white spray.

When Tamina reached the Earl's stateroom, she found him already seated at his desk, apparently busy writing, his dark hair falling across his forehead, a smear of ink on his fingers.

He looked up as she entered and half rose as the ship tilted and Tamina almost ran down the cabin towards the desk.

Laughing she managed to brace herself against the brass rail of the desk as the *Blue Diamond* righted itself once more.

But she noticed there was no answering smile on the Earl's face as he sank back into his leather chair.

He looked stern and remote and suddenly Tamina

was glad she had not insisted that Joe told him about Nancy.

"I fear we are in for a rough time, my Lord," she ventured, sliding into her seat, glad that the chair was bolted firmly to the floor, obviously prepared for such an eventuality.

The Earl busied himself with his notes.

His secretary looked flushed and bright-eyed.

No doubt Miss Waites had spent her luncheon break talking with the fresh-faced young Lieutenant Oxburn.

Well, it made *no* difference to him!

He was just disappointed that, although she had seemed like an honourable girl, here she was flirting with the first man she met on board.

"Did your Officer friend tell you how long we can expect the storm to last?" he asked briefly.

Tamina looked up from her notebook, puzzled.

"Officer friend? Oh, do you mean the Lieutenant Oxburn?"

The Earl leant back in his chair, his strong tanned hand fidgeting with the lid of the heavy silver inkwell.

"The very young man who obviously finds you so attractive, Miss Waites. Yes, Lieutenant Oxburn."

Tamina felt hot colour flood up her face. There was a note of disdain in his voice that she found distressing.

She had wondered if the Earl would suspect her of flirting when she had literally thrown herself into the Officer's arms to stop him seeing Joe disappearing through the forbidden hatchway.

She felt tears begin to prick her eyes.

Until she had lost it, she had no idea just how much

this man's good opinion meant to her.

She would have given anything to have explained the circumstances, but there was no way she could do so without giving away Joe's and Nancy's secret. And she had promised them she would not do so.

Tamina knew she had many faults, but she had never in her life broken a promise and she never would.

She took a deep breath, her fingernails pressing hard into her palms.

"Lieutenant Oxburn is a very kind young man and has been very helpful, but I am sure I mean no more to him than any other passenger."

The Earl shrugged.

"If you say so, Miss Waites, then of course I accept your statement. And anyway, as long as it does not affect your work, your social life is of no concern to me! Now, shall we begin?"

Tamina bit her lip, bent her head and began to take down the notes he was dictating.

She was angry inside, wondering if he had known that he was talking to Lady Tamina Braithwaite, he would never have dreamed of saying such hurtful words.

For the next hour they worked without exchanging any other comments except those concerned with his book.

But Tamina was only too well aware that the motion of the ship was growing even more violent and eventually as it tilted, rolled and shook itself back again, the Earl looked up and for a moment concern shone in his dark eyes.

Then the stern expression returned as he suggested, "I think we should stop now, Miss Waites. The storm is gathering strength. I think it would be wise if you retired to your cabin for the evening. I doubt if the Captain will now be hosting his function so you probably brought your ball gown with you for no good reason!"

Tamina caught back a little gasp at his sarcasm, but she was determined to remain dignified.

She thanked him quietly and made her way out of the room.

The tears she had been fighting all afternoon finally spilled down her cheeks and she leaned against the wall of the corridor, battling to get herself under control.

Fresh air! That was what she needed.

It was so stuffy below decks, even though it was cold and damp, she felt she could not breathe.

She now staggered along the corridor and up the stairway, clutching the brass rail as the ship rolled wildly, first to port then to starboard.

There was no one around. Even the hardiest souls had retired to their cabins, but an atmosphere of unease and concern hung over the big ship as it ploughed through the rough seas.

For an instant Tamina wondered if she should return to her cabin. But stubbornly she refused to give in – she would not be denied her fresh air!

At last she reached the door to the deck and tugged hard at the handle, but it would not move and she realised it was the pressure of the wind that was holding it shut.

Bracing herself, she pulled with all her strength and managed to force it open far enough to slide out.

The power of the storm took her by surprise.

She found herself staggering along the deck, her hair flying free of its clips as the wind howled in across the waves crashing against the side of the *Blue Diamond*.

Gulping for breath and soaked to the skin, Tamina managed to break her headlong flight at last by linking her arm round a metal post. She gazed out at the angry ocean, scared but awed by the sight.

It was nearly dark but there was just enough light for her to see a vast expanse of grey sea with giant waves crested in white and yellow foam roaring towards the ship, driven on by a gale force wind that never ceased.

Spray thundered over the deck, soaking her to the skin and suddenly she felt afraid.

She had not realised how dangerous it would be to come on deck when such a storm was raging.

And the vessel that had seemed so large when she had boarded it in Southampton, now appeared very small and helpless against this ferocious attack by nature at its very worst.

Tamina would never have believed that such a great ship could be thrown around like a toy in a child's bath.

She shuddered and was glad that the lifeboat drill had been accomplished so well on the first day they had sailed.

But looking down on the terrible sea, she realised that the small lifeboats would stand no chance even if they could be launched.

Water crashed across the deserted deck and Tamina felt her hold on the metal post loosen. She groaned and clung on desperately. Surely this violent motion could not go on for ever?

A thrill of fear ran across her body – the doorway back to the covered deck seemed miles away. She was unsure if she could reach it safely.

She could die out here in the cold and dark, tossed like a rag doll into the cruel raging water, and she could only imagine how devastated her parents would feel – if they even ever discovered what her fate had been.

Tamina now realised that she had been extremely foolhardy, putting herself into such danger unnecessarily.

Throughout her short life she had been protected, sheltered and cared for. Even when her older brothers had thoughtlessly risked their lives during their madcap games, they had always been there to help her out of trouble.

She had taken their protection for granted.

But now on this storm-tossed sea she was *alone*, completely alone.

Carelessly she had never imagined a situation she could not cope with.

'This is all my fault!' she thought desperately. 'If I had not been so full of my own self-pity when Edmund betrayed me, I would not have run away. I did not stop to think through the problem and now that same fault has left me in dreadful danger.'

But as yet another wave crashed over her, Tamina forced her mind to work faster.

She gathered together all her courage and resolve. She would worry over the shortcomings of her character and behaviour when she was safely back inside the ship.

She dashed the icy salt water from her eyes and carefully measured the distance along the deck to the next stanchion she could grasp.

Then as a huge wave washed back over the rails, she flung herself forward, gaining a useful yard towards the half open door.

Suddenly a shape filled the doorway and a figure fought its way along the deck towards her.

"Miss Waites!"

It was the Earl.

Jacketless, his new lawn shirt already soaked and clinging to his chest, he reached out a hand and with a cry of relief, Tamina grabbed it.

"Oh – my Lord, I am – *so* thankful to see you!"

His arms went around her and he half pulled, half carried her back along the deck and inside the covered passageway.

"Good Heavens! *You stupid girl*! You could have been killed! Whatever possessed you to go out on deck in this weather?"

Tamina leant against him for a moment as the ship rolled savagely once more, feeling the warm relief of his strength that had saved her from the elements.

Reluctantly she pulled herself upright and out of his powerful encircling arms.

"Thank you, my Lord – I am so grateful to you. I fear I sadly misjudged the conditions – it was my own fault for being stubborn. I wanted fresh air and was determined to find it at any cost!"

She gazed up at him, not realising how attractive she looked with her long golden hair darkened to rich amber by the salt water. Drops glistened on her eyelashes and her cheeks were whipped to rose by the cold and wind.

The Earl caught his breath.

He had never seen anyone so lovely.

The dark blue of her eyes, the funny little nose.

He desperately wanted to kiss her and even bent his

head towards hers, but his commonsense came to his rescue.

Before he had been interrupted by events in his cabin, he had meant to find Miss Waites and apologise for his unpardonable rudeness.

He had been shocked at his own behaviour. Being sarcastic to a member of his staff who could not answer back was unforgivable.

And that was what he had to remember – that Miss Waites was an employee of his – a young unprotected woman in his care.

It would be a hellish thing to do, to take advantage of such a girl, even though his feelings for her were now growing stronger every day.

"We all do foolish things sometimes, Miss Waites," he remarked dryly and she wondered if she had misheard the humour in his voice.

"Why were you looking for me, my Lord? Have you more work for me to undertake?"

"No, no. It is far too rough to work. I came to tell you that poor Joe has taken a nasty fall and given his head a bad knock against the side of one of the trunks. He is at present in the infirmary cabin being attended by the ship's doctor."

"Oh, that's awful. Poor Joe. Is he conscious?"

"He slips in and out, but he will not settle to rest and seems very distressed. The doctor wants him to sleep, but we cannot calm him. He is calling for you, Miss Waites."

"For me?"

They had reached the doorway to her cabin and Tamina paused, bewildered at the Earl's remarks. Why should Joe need to speak to her? She hardly knew the boy.

Then she remembered it all clearly and to the Earl's astonishment she flung open her cabin door and peered inside.

She could tell immediately that no one had been in the room since she was last here.

There was no sign of Joe's fiancée, Nancy.

He must have fallen and hurt himself before he could move her. And that meant that the young girl was still lying down in that cold dangerous stairwell.

Tamina staggered as the boat rocked again. She flung out a hand and the Earl caught it.

"Whatever is wrong, Miss Waites? You look as if you have seen a ghost."

Tamina spun round to him.

All she could see in her mind's eye was that metal platform, so many feet below this deck, a young girl lying there, ill and helpless, sliding perilously close to the edge and a fall to her death on the wicked metal pipes below.

There was no choice.

Whatever it did to their relationship, she would have to tell the Earl and confess that she and Joe had deceived him!

CHAPTER SEVEN

Tamina became conscious that she had been staring into the Earl's dark eyes for long silent minutes without speaking.

Her pulse was racing and she felt a little faint.

She realised she knew this man so well even though they had spent such a short time in each other's company.

She knew him far better than she had ever known Edmund.

The Earl was going to be so disappointed to learn that she and Joe had deceived him in such a way.

To lose his respect and liking, even if it was just the liking an employer had for an employee would be really devastating.

Tamina mentally shook herself and took a deep breath.

There was no time to waste in worrying about her own emotions and feelings.

She had to rescue Nancy.

"My Lord, I have to ask you to accompany me below decks?"

The Earl's dark brows now drew together in an astonished frown.

"I beg your pardon!"

"Oh, please, *please*, follow me. I need your help immediately. The explanations must wait."

The Earl nodded at once, impressed by the passion he saw in her blue eyes and startled by the air of command assumed by his usually mild-mannered secretary.

Without speaking he followed her back along the corridor and to his surprise, as the boat rocked violently, Miss Waites opened a small metal door and then hurried through.

Intrigued the Earl followed her, catching back a cry of alarm as she vanished abruptly down a steep metal ladder into the gloom.

He began to shout a warning, but caught his breath sharply as he saw what appeared to be the body of a young boy in a green uniform clinging to the metal steps below.

Miss Waites was crouching by her side, trying to raise his head from the metal deck and looking up, her huge blue eyes seemed almost dark as midnight in this cold fetid space between decks.

"Dammit, who is this poor boy? What is he doing here?"

The Earl clattered down the steps and then gulped.

As he carefully lifted the body into his arms, he realised by the flowing red hair cascading across him that this was no boy – this was a young woman, no more than sixteen or seventeen years of age.

Grimly he noticed too that the rug she had thrown off her in her illness was one of his own travelling blankets!

"Explanations later, Miss Waites! This wretched child is frozen with the cold."

He carried her swiftly up the ladder, bracing himself easily against the rocking of the ship.

Tamina followed him.

She was so glad to get out of that freezing metal tomb. The sound of the storm was so loud down there, the crashing of the endless waves against the side of the ship magnified a thousand times over.

She shuddered.

Of course a ship this size could never sink, never be rolled over by the huge waves, but all she could imagine was what it would be like if the ship began to founder and she and the Earl were trapped below decks.

When she reached the warm corridor, the Earl was standing, hesitating.

"Quickly, take her to my cabin," urged Tamina and hurried ahead to open the door.

Staggering against the rolling of the vessel, the Earl carried Nancy inside and laid her down on the bed.

The young woman gave a little sigh and began to regain consciousness.

"I shall summon the medical staff immediately," announced the Earl tersely.

Without thinking Tamina shot out her hand and grasped his arm.

"No, wait!"

Then seeing the surprise on his face at her tone of voice, which had been of someone speaking to an equal in rank, she continued,

"I am sorry, my Lord, I did not mean to speak so rudely, but if we call the doctor to attend to her, I think she will be imprisoned somewhere on the ship and probably your valet will be as well!"

The Earl turned his dark gaze on her and Tamina realised with a sinking heart that he was looking stern and distant.

"Obviously there is a story here that I have to be told. I will wait in my cabin and be grateful if you would come to me as soon as is possible."

He then gave her a brief nod and departed, the door closing behind him with ominous finality.

Tamina bit her lip as she hurried to help Nancy out of the wet uniform. She wrapped the girl in a thick dressing gown and dried her long red hair as much as she could.

"Oh, miss, thank you so much. Oh, dear, what's goin' to 'appen now? Where's my Joe? Does he know the Earl found me? Will he be turned away? Oh, miss, 'e'll be that upset if he loses his position. He's so proud to be carrying on the job his brother had. Oh, it'll all be my fault!"

Big tears ran down her face and Tamina took her hand and spoke forcefully but kindly, trying to remember that she was Miss Waites and not Lady Tamina.

"Nonsense, now don't distress yourself, Nancy. Joe had a little accident but he will be fine. He fell and hit his head and that is why he could not come to you himself.

"When the storm became so very violent, I felt it only right that I had to break my promise and tell the Earl about you – for your own safety."

Nancy wiped the tears away.

"What will 'appen to us now, miss? Will I be arrested for stowin' away?"

Tamina shook her head in a decisive fashion, her blue eyes sparkling.

"No, what I intend to do is approach the Captain and say that you are my maid, that you were supposed to stay at home, but stupidly followed me on board with a message and became scared when the ship sailed. You hid on the stairwell, but now have confessed. No one needs to know about the disguise! I will throw the uniform out of the porthole tonight!"

"Oh, miss!"

"I will offer to pay for your passage. There is room in here to make you up a bed and it will only be until we reach Madeira. There you and Joe must make your own arrangements to send you home, but I am sure the Earl will help. He is a caring employer and for all his stern appearance, a kind man."

"Oh, miss, you are *so* kind to me!"

And then bidding Nancy rest for a while, Tamina left her cabin, knowing she would now have to face the Earl and hear his judgement on her behaviour.

When she reached his stateroom, Tamina found him pacing up and down, rubbing his wet hair with a towel.

His shirt was open at the neck and he had discarded his coat that was lying in a soggy heap on the floor.

Without thinking Tamina bent to pick it up to hang it over the back of a chair.

"Leave it!" snapped the Earl. "Joe can deal with it."

Tamina bit her lip.

"Has Joe recovered, my Lord?"

"Yes, once I told him that his fiancée was safe, he relaxed and fell asleep. The doctor assures me he will regain all his abilities when he awakes, except for a bad headache."

Tamina continued to straighten out the cabin.

There were so many books, clothes and papers scattered everywhere. The rolling of the great ship had caused havoc with the work lying on the Earl's desk. Several pages were covered in ink where a particularly vicious roll had caused an inkwell to open and flood across the top.

"Miss Waites, I asked you to stop! I would like you to tell me what you know of this – this – deception. Were you in on the plan from the beginning?"

The Earl jammed his fists into his trouser pockets and then glared at Tamina. The thought that this girl had blatantly deceived him in such a fashion had disturbed him in ways he did not fully understand.

He would have wagered good money that she was not the type to do so, but perhaps he was wrong, he thought bitterly. Perhaps all women were capable of such deceptions.

He recalled the honeyed words of Lady Eunice when they had met only a few weeks ago.

How he had felt comforted by her sympathy for the loss of his family, how he had nearly given her his heart, been about to ask her to marry him, until he discovered she belonged to another man.

He still could not believe a lady of breeding and good family like Eunice had been able to take part in a deceit of such deep gravity.

He had lain awake, night after night, trying to work out why and how he had been taken in by her charms.

Now he struggled to keep his temper.

Was this Miss Waites just such a woman as well? And why did it matter so much to him?

Tamina felt hot colour flood into her cheeks.

She had expected the Earl to be annoyed, but not this angry. She was only an employee after all and not a close friend.

And she hated to think that he could hold such a poor opinion of her.

"My Lord, I had hoped that you would know a little of my character by now. I would never have agreed to such a reckless plan or deceived you by plotting with Joe and Nancy. You have shown me nothing but kindness and courtesy. I could *never* repay you in such a way."

He heard her words, but could not quell the feelings that coursed through him.

He could still picture that treacherous and slippery metal stairway that ran between the decks. The tossing of the ship could have thrown her off into the well that ran right to the lowest decks.

Miss Waites was so small and slight, although he had to admit she was braver than any other female he had ever known.

Tamina explained swiftly when she had learned about Nancy and how she had planned to sort out the problem.

"So you still did not mean to tell me!"

She tossed her head.

"Until we reached Madeira – yes. There I thought the problem could be resolved. Joe would tell you about Nancy and with your help arrange for her to obtain work on the island, hopefully with a family who would give her a passage home with them at some point in the future."

The Earl took a step towards her.

"And did you not stop to think for one second that you were putting yourself in great danger climbing up and down inside the ship? What would have happened if you had slipped and fallen?"

"My Lord, I am not some weak and feeble female who does not dare venture into a difficult situation if called to do so! I have two older brothers who would have scoffed and laughed at me if I had declined to investigate out of cowardice."

The Earl frowned.

"Miss Waites, you must promise me that you will never do such a thing again!"

"My Lord, although you are my employer, I cannot possibly make such a promise!"

The Earl took another step forward and grasped her shoulders.

How dare she be so flippant? Did her life mean so little to her?

He stared down into her flushed face, his gaze fixed on the beautiful lips so close to his.

He felt an overwhelming desire to kiss her.

Tamina gasped.

The Earl's fingers were tight on her shoulders and as she stared up into the handsome face, she had the strangest feeling that he was about to kiss her.

And she knew without a doubt that she would let him!

Then came a flash of uncertainty in the Earl's eyes and he loosened his grip and turned away from her.

He busied himself tearing up the ink-soaked notes on his desk and throwing them in the waste-paper basket.

Suddenly he turned back to Tamina.

"You are quite right, of course, Miss Waites. But as

I am your employer for the duration of this trip, perhaps we can agree that you will do as little as you possibly can to partake of activities that might hinder the completion of my book. If your madcap behaviour meant a stay in hospital, I might then have difficulty in finding another secretary in Madeira. And that would be – *inconvenient*."

And with that he walked into his bedroom cabin and closed the door.

Tamina bit her lip and dug her nails hard into the palms of her hands.

The Earl had sounded irritable, almost bored. What had she been imagining?

Obviously she had been completely wrong about his desire to kiss her!

What a silly little fool she was to think that this marvellous man would take any interest in a Miss Tabitha Waites, a lowly secretary, when he had all the eligible Society ladies of England willing to become his wife.

But, oh, how good it would feel to tell him *exactly* who she was.

She knew that her emotions had been stirred and captured by the Earl in a way she had never imagined could happen to her.

She longed to be in his company the whole time.

She listened for his voice, admired his talent for writing, his sense of honour and his dedication in taking over as head of the family when he had been so devastated by his brother's tragic death.

Tamina had never met a man who interested her so much.

Even their sense of humour seemed the same. Little light jokes he had made during their time together had convinced her of that.

Now Tamina turned away and began to gather up the notes that had escaped the ink damage. She would go back to her cabin and write them up neatly. At least she could still be of some help to him.

She could hardly see, her eyes filling with stupid tears.

So this was what true love felt like?

She now shuddered. The feelings she had held for Edmund were nothing in comparison to those that were coursing through her now.

It was like comparing the flicker of a candle flame to the roaring of a great fire.

Once – and incredibly she realised it was only a few days ago – she had scrubbed her mouth to remove the memory of Edmund's kiss.

Now, oh, how she would have welcomed the touch of the Earl's lips on hers!

*

During the long night the storm abated.

Tamina hardly slept and at five in the morning she was sitting, staring out of her porthole as the dawn broke and she could see that the angry seas had vanished.

Washing and dressing quickly in a demure cream top and skirt, she stepped over Nancy's still sleeping form, bundled up in travelling rugs on the floor.

She stopped for a second as she pulled a cloak with a silk hood over her outfit and stared down at the stowaway.

She was really such a pretty young girl with wild corkscrews of flaming red cascading across the cushion under her head.

In her sleep the worry lines had vanished from her face and the dreadful pallor had gone. There was a little pink in her cheeks now and she was half smiling.

Tamina wondered if she was dreaming of her fiancé, Joe.

As she left her cabin and made her way along the companionway towards the deck, she realised she felt a certain envy of young Nancy.

To love and know you are loved in return. Was there any greater gift in life? Any greater joy?

Tamina knew her parents and brothers loved her, but that was not the same as knowing you had the affection and respect of a man you could call your soulmate.

That you stirred ecstatic passion in him as he did for you.

She realised now that what she had felt for Edmund had just been a young girl's wish to *be* in love. It had nothing to do with falling *in* love at all.

On deck she discovered that the wind had dropped. The sky was a pale duck-egg blue and the air tasted like sweet white wine.

Even though it was still so early, there were several people already up and about, well wrapped up in rugs, sipping an early morning cup of coffee.

Tamina strolled along the deck, pleased to feel the light breeze on her skin. She took deep breaths of the glorious air and felt her spirits lift slightly.

She was by nature an optimistic girl and although she had no idea what was going to happen to her, she faced the new day with hope.

She had been leaning on the rail, gazing down at the

dark green waters, delighted to see a shoal of dolphins keeping up with the great boat, when a voice came from behind her.

"I see the storm has passed, Miss Waites."

She spun round to find the Earl standing behind her.

He was smiling and with a great feeling of relief, Tamina realised that his black mood of the night before had vanished with the new day.

"A new day and a new start, my Lord," she said mischievously, her blue eyes sparkling up into his.

His lips twitched.

"Indeed. And – look – you can see the tip of the island of Madeira on the horizon!"

With a sigh of delight, Tamina followed his pointing finger and yes, there on the hard blue line that divided the ocean from the sky, was a speck of black.

"Will we reach port today?"

To her surprise, the Earl shook his head.

"No, I have been told by Captain Reid that we have suffered some minor damage to the propeller during the storm. We are under way, as you can see, but we won't be making landfall until tomorrow morning."

He laughed and leaning over the rail, pointed down to where the dolphins were diving and rolling under and through the wake of the *Blue Diamond*.

"Your slippery friends down there will reach the harbour before we do. We like to think we can better nature and God's creatures, but they show us we are far frailer than we imagine – especially at sea!"

Tamina stared out towards the far horizon.

They had another whole day on board before all the

formalities of land surrounded them.

There would be all the problems to sort out today regarding Nancy, but when that was done she knew she would spend her time with the Earl of Daventry.

And no matter what they did, she knew she would treasure every moment with him as if it was her last.

The Earl glanced down at the tiny person standing next to him, her bright blonde hair streaming in the wind.

The hood of her cloak had slipped back from her face and the long curls were fighting again to escape from their clips and pins.

It was strange but he had to admit that Miss Waites was not too accomplished when it came to dressing her hair in that severe style. Which was very odd when you remembered she had to do it every day.

It was just one more part of the puzzle surrounding his secretary.

He stared out across the ocean at the first sighting of Madeira.

There would be another twenty-four hours before they reached the fascinating port of Funchal.

He realised he was looking forward to this day. He wanted to sit and watch Miss Waites's face as they came closer and closer to the island.

There was an enjoyment of life in this bright young girl that he had never experienced in any of his more sophisticated friends.

"Breakfast, Miss Waites?" he enquired cheerfully and offered her his arm in a light-hearted cavalier fashion.

And with a laugh Tamina accepted. Tomorrow and all the problems it would bring could definitely wait.

CHAPTER EIGHT

The midday sun blazed down on the narrow hilly streets of Funchal, the Capital of the beautiful island of Madeira.

The low white buildings dozed behind their blue shutters. The lanes and alleyways were deserted with only lazy bees bumbling around through the cascades of pink and purple bougainvillea and other brilliantly-coloured flowers that dropped a profuse confetti of petals onto the cobblestones below.

A lonely figure trudged uphill along one wide road in a fashionable area of the town.

Joe stopped for a moment in the shade of a tree that to his amazement was growing real lemons to wipe the sweat from his shining face with a big red handkerchief.

Under the floppy white hat the Earl had given him to wear, his blond hair was sticking to his forehead and irritating the scar that was just beginning to heal under its bandage.

He stared back down the dusty road – from this elevated position he could see the harbour spread out below him. The vessels clustered around the docks looked tiny, like a small child's bath-time toys.

He could just make out the shape of the *Blue*

Diamond where it sat snugly against the dock.

The sea looked very blue, flat and calm and it was hard to remember that, only a few days ago, it had been a maelstrom of towering waves and vicious icy spray.

He could not remember falling and hitting his head, only how kind the Earl and Miss Waites had been to him when he finally came round.

It had been such a relief to know that Nancy was well and being taken care of. He loved her so much and felt guilty that he had caused her so much grief.

'What if she 'ad died down there in that 'orrid 'ole between the decks!' he muttered to himself. 'It would have been my fault for makin' her run away with me.

'My Lord was quite right – 'e said I should have spoken to 'im about it and he would have dealt with her Dad, that old devil Rider. He said Jacob would have told his brother and so I should have trusted 'im to do what was right for me and Nancy.'

The sun was burning his fair English skin.

Joe sighed.

He would have given a lot to sit in the shade for a few minutes, but he knew he did not have the time to relax.

The Earl had given him the afternoon off, but he was due back on board the *Blue Diamond* in the evening.

Joe now had to admit that the Earl had been very considerate. So many employers would have thrown him out without a reference.

When he had finally recovered his wits after hitting his head during the storm, Joe had discovered that they had docked at Funchal and Nancy was gone from the *Blue Diamond*!

This morning Miss Waites had given him a little note that Nancy had written before she left the ship.

"You are not to worry, Joe," the Earl's secretary had said, her voice soft and calming. "His Lordship has found Nancy a position with a family who are renting a villa in Madeira for the summer and they will be returning to England in October. She will be perfectly safe until you can meet up once more."

"Thank you, miss! His Lordship gave me a long lecture about 'ow stupid we'd been and Nancy could have died without your 'elp. I'll never be able to repay you."

He liked Miss Waites, but the small golden-haired girl baffled him.

She was only an employee and about his age, but her air of authority and the way she spoke and carried herself told Joe that she came from a much higher social level.

Joe had seen the way the Earl looked at her, when Miss Waites was not aware.

He realised he felt sorry for the man who seemed to have so much in the way of power, position and wealth, because an alliance between the two of them would never work.

At least his love for Nancy was returned and one day they would be happy together.

Nancy's note had said that he was not to worry about her, but Joe was determined to speak to the girl he loved so much before the *Blue Diamond* put to sea again.

'I'm not goin' to sail away to other foreign parts until I talk to my Nancy,' he muttered now as he walked on until he reached a large villa, set well back from the road in its own shady grounds.

"*Vil - la Mi - mo - sa,*" he mumbled, reading the dark

blue lettering on the white name tile sunk into one of the gate pillars.

'That's the place where the Earl told me 'e had found a position for Nancy. Well, it's a fine lookin' house and no mistake.'

Pushing open the ornate iron gates, he made his way up a long tree-shaded gravel drive round to the back of the house to where the kitchen door stood open.

And luck was on his side!

There was Nancy, her red hair tied up under a big white cap sitting on a chair in the sunshine shelling peas.

"*Joe!*"

Her pretty heart-shaped face lit up with delight and then she threw a scared glance over her shoulder.

"You shouldn't be 'ere! There'll be trouble if you're found."

"I wasn't goin' to sail away without makin' sure you were all right, my sweetheart!"

Nancy put down the basin of peas and taking his hand hurried across the sun-baked courtyard to a small storeroom where piles of vegetables were stacked.

She picked up a shallow wicker basket and began to fill it with onions and tomatoes.

"Oh, Joe, it's so lovely to see you, but I'll get into fearful trouble if we're caught!"

Joe reached out and took the basket from her grasp. He put it down, caught her hands in his and pulled her towards him for a kiss.

"Nancy! Oh, it's so wonderful to see you. Are they treatin' you right? The Earl told me they were a good family, but if you're un'appy – "

"No, no. I'm all right, Joe."

She squeezed his fingers and gazed up into his serious blue eyes.

"They're just very strict, that's all, and the other servants are all from this island and don't speak a lot of English, so it's a bit lonely. But I'm learnin' odd words of Portuguese!

"I have to do all sorts of work – in the kitchen, servin' on table, cleanin' silver. It seems the Master and Mistress are quite careful with their money. I think they were pleased to get an English servant cheaply. But I'm just so thankful that the Earl didn't have me arrested for stowin' away."

"Who's in the family?"

"A Mr. and Mrs. Simmons and her elderly parents. I don't see them much. They keep to their rooms. Mrs. Simmons is very strict, but fair. I don't like 'er 'usband much. He's always abrupt and rude, findin' fault with everythin'. He's a businessman. Owns a lot of factories in England and America. Somethin' to do with biscuits and sweets, I think."

Joe wasn't that interested in what Mr. Simmons did.

"But they will surely take you 'ome with them in October?"

"Oh, yes. They've already booked passage for the first week. And I'm goin' too. I think the Earl insisted."

Joe felt a wave of relief flood over him.

"He's a good man and I reckon that Miss Waites played a part in it all too."

"She was really nice to me, so she was. Now, Joe Goodall, you get back to the boat quick, afore someone comes lookin' for me."

He bent his head and gave her another shy kiss.

"One day we'll be together all the time, Nancy. I promise!"

She smiled at him and picking up the basket led him cautiously across the courtyard and round the corner of the villa.

"Oh, Joe, one really strange thing. Mr. and Mrs. Simmons have a visitor, a Mr. Newson. He arrived on a fast steamer from England the day before we got 'ere. A young gentleman in politics, so the kitchen staff say."

"A young man? He 'asn't – said anythin' to you – suggested – ?"

Nancy waved away his words impatiently.

"No, no, nothin' like that. But when I was dustin' the library this mornin', I was down on my knees behind a big bookcase and I over'eard him talking to that Mr. Simmons.

"He said he was plannin' to marry a rich girl because it would further his career."

Joe frowned.

"What's so strange about that, sweetheart? Lots of men try to marry rich girls to get on in life."

"I know that, but listen, this Mr. Simmons, he said, 'is she keen on the match?' and Mr. Newson replied, 'no, I think she loathes me at the moment, but I have no doubt that once she has spent the night with me, she will see the error of her ways!' And they laughed."

Nancy shuddered. She could still hear the menace and cold cruelty in that laughter, but knew she would never be able to explain to dear straightforward Joe, how scared it had made her feel.

Although Joe had lived in the same poor area as her

112

family, the Goodalls had always been in work, a little extra money had meant that their lives were not spent wondering where the penny for the rent was coming from.

Nancy knew that because of her father's habits of drinking and gambling, she knew more about the seedy side of life than her dear naïve Joe.

"It was 'orrid. Really nasty. I wondered just who the poor girl was that he was going to betray in such a fashion."

Joe sighed and gave her a brief hug.

"I expect it *was* 'orrid, Nan. But that's quality folks for you. She won't be anyone we know, now will she? So best you just forget it. You do your work, stay quietly in the background and keep out of this man's way."

"I'll do that, don't you fear, Joe. The family are goin' away this evening to stay with some friends for the weekend. Mr. Newson will be 'ere in the 'ouse by 'imself, but I'm not going to answer the bell if it rings! I'll get Manuel, the footman, to go instead."

By now they had reached the main gates of the Villa Mimosa. Suddenly the crack of a whip and the clatter of hooves on the gravel made them spin round.

A horse and rider were coming down the drive from the house. Nancy pulled Joe into the shelter of a great tree.

"Look, Joe! That's that Mr. Newson I was tellin' you of."

Joe peered through the branches.

He could see the man clearly – young, fair-haired and good-looking, but he was using the whip on his horse too much and Joe reckoned he had a cruel streak in him.

They watched as he kicked the poor animal into a

canter and vanished down the road towards Funchal.

"Nasty lookin' bloke!" said Joe. "You mind you steer well clear of 'im, Nancy, my girl. You're right – I feel sorry for the young lady who he means to trap into marryin' him but, then, there's nothin' we can do about it, now is there?

"Now, give us a kiss and I'll be getting' back to the old boat. His Lordship has been explorin' the Flower Market today, but 'e'll want me to be back on board to 'elp him get ready for dinner, I reckon."

And he clasped her in his arms wondering when he would see her again.

*

Tamina decided this was the happiest time of her life.

For three days she had been so busy. Once the *Blue Diamond* had reached Funchal, she had been involved in the tricky problem of Nancy's presence on board.

This problem had meant an interview with a rather irate Captain, but luckily the Earl's position in Society had meant that on payment of a steerage class ticket, Nancy officially became a passenger.

Then Tamina had been proud and thrilled when the Earl had wanted her advice as to the suitability of the young girl for a position working for an English family on the island.

She had been swift to assure him that Nancy would make a good kitchen maid and a natural intelligence that could with training be put to use in a higher position still in a large household.

This morning the Earl had been discussing the outcome of the problem and laughed as he finished

114

signing the letters he had dictated to Tamina earlier.

One of them had been to the Agency that had placed Nancy in her new job with a family called Simmons who were renting a villa in Funchal for the summer and were keen to employ an English-speaking maid.

"You seem to have a good knowledge of how these domestic affairs are conducted, Miss Waites?"

Tamina had felt a blush rise into her cheeks. She had forgotten for the moment that she was only a secretary and not a lady of means and station being groomed to run her own household.

"I have – observed in various large houses where I have worked – how these things are done, my Lord."

"You have observed very well indeed and I must compliment you on the way you have dealt with Joe's young woman. I feared hysteria, a lot of crying and some dreadful scene when she had to leave the ship."

Tamina had shaken her head.

"No, my Lord, you were mistaken. Nancy is young, I admit, but very much in love with her Joe."

"You believe in the power of love?"

Tamina's dark blue eyes grew large and dreamy.

"Oh, yes, my Lord. I truly do."

There was a long silence and she realised she had been staring up at him without guarding her expression.

She was horrified to think what emotions he had seen written on her face and carried on hastily,

"Nancy is also well possessed of a great deal of commonsense. She knows that Joe will marry her one day and will wait patiently for that time to arrive.

"She also realises just how lucky she has been that

you persuaded the Captain not to take any action against them. She is thankful for your Lordship's forbearance, as indeed am I."

The Earl frowned.

A moment ago he had looked into her eyes and believed he saw a depth of feeling for him from a woman he had only ever dreamed would be his.

Then she had controlled herself and now he glanced at Tamina, his dark eyes serious.

For a moment he looked almost hurt.

"Surely you did not believe I would have cast the poor young woman ashore without a thought?"

Tamina took an impulsive step forward, her hand going out to him.

Then swiftly she pulled it back. It was not her place to offer sympathy.

"Of course not, my Lord. I was never in any doubt as to the course of action you would take."

The Earl sighed.

"Because of my rank and position in the world, I suppose."

"No, because you are a *good man*," whispered Tamina, the colour deepening in her cheeks.

A warm smile broke across the handsome serious face in front of her and, for a moment, she thought the Earl was going to reach out and clasp her hand.

But the moment passed and instead he said,

"I think after our hard work this morning we are entitled to an afternoon at leisure, Miss Waites. I have given Joe the time off and cannot see that we should work while others play. Would you care to explore Funchal a little? I think you will find it extremely interesting."

An hour later they were walking down the gangway into the exciting and colourful expanse of Funchal harbour.

Tamina had dressed simply for their expedition in a crisp white and lemon dress which was reserved and respectable with a high neck and long sleeves.

But in the rush to leave England and get away from Edmund, she had quite forgotten to pack a sensible parasol and was unaware that the frilly white sunshade that she carried cast enchanting patterns across her face.

As Tamina walked by the Earl's side, she tilted back the parasol so she could glance up at him.

The Earl caught his breath.

Her deep sapphire eyes were sparkling in the bright sunshine and when the shadow fell across her forehead, he had the oddest notion that he had seen that charming gaze somewhere before – in quite another place –

"You approve of Funchal, Miss Waites?"

"Oh, it is just quite marvellous, my Lord. The picturesque buildings, the many quaint cobbled streets, the lemon trees – and the flowers! I cannot believe the amazing colours and scents."

She gazed around in thrilled delight at the cascades of roses and lilies. Strange orange and blue blooms that the Earl told her were bird of paradise flowers. And everywhere great trailing bunches of bougainvillea and hibiscus.

Every shape and colour and scent was present and Tamina felt giddy with the beauty surrounding her.

"This is the famous Flower Market. It is at its best early in the morning, of course, but still magnificent."

Tamina gasped and ran forward to a stall selling huge bunches of a small fluffy yellow flower.

"Oh, look, mimosa. I adore mimosa!"

The gnarled stall-keeper gave them a toothless grin and broke off a piece.

With a sweeping bow he presented it to the Earl.

"Um presente para sua esposa bonita!"

Laughing the Earl took it. He definitely was not going to tell the old man that Miss Tabitha Waites was not his wife!

Then with all the force of a sudden lightning strike, he realised that that was exactly what he wanted her to be!

He did not care that she was only a simple working girl. She was honest, brave and loyal and *he loved her.*

He was certainly aware that marrying his secretary would cause a huge scandal, but the rest of the world could go hang. Regardless of her station in life, he wanted Tabitha Waites to be *his wife.*

Tamina turned from where she was examining a stall covered in tiny pots of violets and pansies.

"What did he say?" she asked cheerfully. "I fear his accent is far removed from the classical Portuguese I know."

The Earl shook his head. Now was not the time to speak. He would wait until they were back on board the *Blue Diamond.*

He would plan a dinner for the two of them and then perhaps during a moonlit walk on the deck, he would propose.

"A gift for the beautiful lady," he said and wove the short stems of the mimosa between the lace panels of her parasol.

"Thank you, my Lord."

She smiled up at him, thinking how lovely it was to see his stern face relaxed and happy.

The lines of grief and worry were now fading from around his eyes and when she saw the warmth of feeling in his gaze, a tremor of love and desire shot through her veins.

Could the Earl possibly be thinking of her in the same way she thought of him?

Oh! Life could not be so good, so perfect. For her to win this man's love and trust would be so amazing.

"I have a few small business transactions to attend to," the Earl was saying as they left the Flower Market. "Will you wait for me here?"

Tamina nodded her head, wishing she could tell him that she would wait for him forever.

She sat on a low stone wall overlooking a pretty little fountain in the centre of a square.

The Earl walked across to a bank to obtain more currency.

As he was leaving, he stood for a moment, gazing across at the slim graceful figure of the woman he loved.

She was leaning across to look down at the pool, dabbling her fingers amongst the pink and yellow water lilies.

Suddenly he was aware of a man in riding jacket and breeches walking in great haste across the square towards Miss Waites.

And before he could move, the man had taken her by her shoulders and seemed to be trying to kiss her!

With a shout, the Earl covered the ground in three great strides and pulled the man away.

119

"What the devil are you doing – !"

The man shook himself free and glared at the Earl.

"Sir, I would suggest it is no concern of yours how a gentleman greets his fiancée!"

The Earl felt the blood in his veins turn to ice.

"*Your fiancée?*"

He stared at the slender girl who had turned very pale.

"Edmund Newson at your service, sir. Yes, I had heard that my fiancée, Lady Tamina Braithwaite, was travelling to Madeira and hoped we would meet up. I am thrilled to have done so in such an unexpected fashion."

"Edmund! I am not – "

"*Lady Tamina Braithwaite!*" the Earl blurted out.

Edmund appeared to look puzzled.

"Why yes. Lady Tamina is the daughter of Lord and Lady Braithwaite. And whom do I have the pleasure of addressing?"

The Earl could hardly hear him for the roaring sound in his ears.

He stared down at Miss Waites – no, Lady Tamina! – and suddenly knew without a doubt that what this man was saying was the truth.

She looked white and guilty, but even as he gazed at her he could see that of course she was a lady of quality.

He remembered that he had thought once that she must have come from a good family, perhaps one that had fallen on hard times.

It was there in her every move, her bearing, the way she spoke.

But lady or not, she had deceived him, lied to him,

pretended to be someone she was not.

Just like Lady Eunice!

He could not believe that he had allowed himself to be tricked once again in this fashion.

And what was worse – he had lost his heart to someone who was completely false.

Why he had been about to propose marriage this evening to a Miss Tabitha Waites, someone who did not even exist! How ridiculous he would have looked.

He was aware that the fair-haired man was waiting for his reply.

"My Lord – " Tamina started to speak piteously, but then stopped with a gasp as he threw out an imperious hand.

"I am Ivan, Lord Daventry."

He then made a short curt bow towards Edmund, centuries of breeding and manners now coming to his aid.

"And now I must take my leave of you, sir. My ship is sailing on the evening tide. Obviously I can leave this young lady, whom I thought was a Miss Waites, my secretary, in your capable hands. *Sir*! *Madam*! Your servant!"

And turning on his heel, he strode off towards the pier.

"My Lord – *wait*! Listen to me!"

Tamina called after him in desperation, but it was no use.

Within seconds he had vanished from sight and she was left, feeling sick and devastated, aware of Edmund's hot clammy hand holding hers.

CHAPTER NINE

Tamina felt a great wave of despair flood over her as she watched the tall figure of the Earl swiftly walk away and vanish down a narrow alleyway leading to the Funchal docks and the *Blue Diamond*.

She knew she would never forget the look in his eyes when he had learnt of what he considered to be her betrayal of his trust.

She turned to Edmund her eyes blazing.

"Edmund, what are you doing here in Madeira? And why did you name me as your fiancée to Lord Daventry? You know I no longer wish to have anything to do with you! I have sent you a letter breaking off our engagement."

Edmund brushed a finger slowly across his thick moustache as he stared down at the beautiful and angry Tamina. His bland, boyish face concealed the rage that was building inside his head.

He had indeed received her letter and had seen all his plans for a moneyed future vanish into thin smoke. Marrying into the esteemed Braithwaite family had seemed like the answer to all his prayers.

Even though he had prospects as a Member of Parliament, Edmund knew his passion for the card tables was going to ruin him unless he could have the use of a great deal of money very quickly.

His relationship with poor Rebecca – the governess who worked for the Mercer family – was also making his life complicated.

He had promised marriage to the silly girl and although he had sworn her to secrecy – as he had Tamina – he was worried that she would tell Lord and Lady Mercer of what she thought would be her future as wife to a politician.

They were rich powerful people and not ones he wanted to alienate before he could make his marriage to the daughter of the Braithwaite family a reality.

Desperate, he had used all his considerable contacts, paid bribes to a few dishonest servants and discovered that Tamina was travelling out to Madeira on board the *Blue Diamond* under an assumed name.

He had intended to send a message to her on board the ship, asking her to meet him.

His plan had been to hurry her away to the Villa Mimosa, to ruin her reputation and force her to marry him.

Edmund's mind was warping under the strain of enormous gambling debts.

Marriage to Tamina had seemed such an easy way out and, as far as he could see, it still was.

He could not understand why she appeared to be working for Lord Daventry, but obviously he had now stumbled on an important secret, hopefully one he could use to his advantage.

"Tamina, my dear, I am deeply sorry if I have upset you in some way," he began, his expression one of sincere boyish bewilderment.

"I was just so very pleased and surprised to see you so unexpectedly here in Funchal. And I apologise for calling you my fiancée, although I must admit I do still have hopes in that direction – No – " he held up a hand as she protested – "I quite understand that you may have changed in your feelings towards me."

"Edmund – I have spoken on the telephone to a young lady whom I believe considers herself betrothed to you. She made it quite plain that you have no real love for me at all and as such I consider any attachment between us to be completely broken."

A dark red flush flooded across Edmund's face and for a second his eyes looked hard and angry. Then he controlled himself and gave her a little bow.

"Of course, Tamina, I accept your decision. I fear I do not fully understand what you are talking about or who the woman is you spoke to, but now is not the time and place to discuss this fully. You look tired and upset. Do you wish me to escort you back to your ship?"

Tamina felt tears well in her eyes.

How could she return to the *Blue Diamond*? It was impossible. She was no longer Miss Tabitha Waites. She had no place on board that vessel any more.

The appalling fact lay in front of her – the Earl considered that she had cheated and fooled him.

The man she thought of so highly who now held her heart and all her dearest affections, but had only contempt for her.

No, Tabitha Waites was now dead. She could only be Lady Tamina from now on and accept that she would never speak to the Earl again in friendship and respect.

"No, I – I do not wish to return to the ship," she

whispered and turned away so Edmund could not see the tears on her cheeks.

But it would have been far better if she had been able to see *his* face.

At that moment a look of evil triumph flashed across it.

"But your luggage – your maid –?"

"I will send for my trunks. I do not have a maid at the moment," responded Tamina quietly.

She could not remember ever feeling so sad or so unhappy in all her life. It was hard to think, to make plans, but she had to find a hotel, arrange for money to be sent from home.

She did not have enough with her to pay for both a hotel and a berth on the next boat back to England.

Edmund clapped his hands together as if he had just had a brilliant idea.

"Why, while your possessions are coming ashore, I suggest you come back to the Villa Mimosa, where I am staying with my good friends, Ernest and Joan Simmons. They are a delightful couple. I am sure they will be only too delighted to welcome you as their guest."

Through a dim mist of despair Tamina heard what Edmund was saying.

It seemed a sensible suggestion. The very thought of finding a respectable hotel, although she guessed that Reids would have a room available for her – but having to explain why she was alone without her luggage was too much to bear.

"If you are sure the Simmons will not object – " she mumbled wearily.

"Certainly they will not. Come, Tamina. My horse

is tethered in the shade over on the other side of the square. If you will consider riding with me, we can soon be back at the villa."

Tamina was hardly aware of his remarks. She allowed him to help her onto the horse and only flinched when his arms tightened possessively around her as he urged the animal into a fast walk.

These arms belonged to a man she had once thought she loved, but now she knew that the only arms she could ever bear to hold her were those of a man who felt nothing for her but contempt!

*

Happy from having seen Nancy, Joe hurried along the corridor and with a polite knock, entered the Earl's cabin.

He had expected it to be empty.

He was sure the Earl and Miss Waites would still be exploring Madeira looking at all the old buildings and Churches the aristocracy always found so interesting.

He had never understood it himself. Churches were fine for being christened, wed and buried, and of course he had the utmost respect for the Parson, but why go just to look at stained glass windows and old stone pillars?

The day cabin was gloomy. The dark heavy curtains were drawn over the portholes to shade the room from the glare of the afternoon sun.

Joe crossed the room to pull them back and then jumped when a voice barked,

"Leave them alone!"

"I'm so sorry, my Lord, I did not see you there."

The Earl was sitting at his desk unmoving, his hands clasped tightly in front of him.

126

Joe hesitated.

He could not see his master's face, but from the tension of his silhouette, he could tell that all was not well.

"Can I get you anythin', my Lord?"

"No."

The word was snapped out and then the Earl sighed, as if remembering his manners and said in a gentler tone,

"No, thank you, Joe. You may take the rest of the evening off. We sail soon, I believe. Perhaps you would like to be on deck to see us leaving."

"Very good, my Lord."

Joe retreated towards the cabin door puzzled. He had already taken his half day off.

This did not make any sense.

The Earl had been in such a good mood earlier. What could have happened to have caused this anger, this distress?

"Oh, and Joe, I expect a message will arrive from – well from someone requesting that Miss Waites's luggage be sent ashore. Please ask one of the chambermaids to pack her bags and make sure they are sent away with all dispatch."

Joe felt his head was spinning.

"Miss Waites is leavin' us, my Lord?"

The Earl laughed and Joe felt the hairs on the back of his neck stand up. It was not a pleasant sound.

"No, Joe, Miss Waites is not leaving us, but Lady Tamina Braithwaite is! It seems we have been somewhat deceived by my ex-secretary. She has met up with her fiancé on the island and her little charade is now at an end."

"Lady Tamina – fiancé – oh!"

"We have been taken for idiots, Joe. Let this be a lesson to you – never trust a woman, especially one who pretends she is loyal to you!"

"Yes, my Lord."

Joe hesitated, one hand on the cabin doorknob.

"No disrespect intended and I'm right sorry if I am talkin' out of turn, but may I say that I always found Miss Waites – I mean, Lady Tamina – to be a generous and 'elpful young lady. She was so kind to my Nancy when she found her.

"I do not dare presume, my Lord, but I'm sure she 'ad a very good reason to pretend to be someone she wasn't."

The Earl stood up abruptly and, with a sharp thrust of his arm, pulled back the curtains over the portholes, letting the late afternoon sun stream into the room.

He stared out to where he could see the sailors preparing to cast off. They would soon be leaving Madeira and his heartbreak behind.

Tamina! How the lovely name suited her. A pretty sparkling name for a beautiful girl with wonderful deep blue eyes.

He thrust his fists into his pockets and suppressed a groan.

He had been about to propose marriage to her.

He had made such big plans including buying her a ring – diamonds and sapphires – to match her eyes.

What would have happened if he had declared his feelings? Offered her his hand? She would have had to confess and then how ridiculous would he have looked?

He sighed deeply.

"Yes, Joe, I expect in the fullness of time I will discover it was some sort of silly game she was playing to entertain herself while she was travelling out here to meet her fiancé.

"Unfortunately some young women have no regard as to the consequences of their careless actions. Anyway, we will soon be sailing and Lady Tamina will surely have a good laugh at my expense in the future with her friends."

"I don't reckon it was any old game, my Lord. Miss Waites – I mean Lady Tamina – worked very hard on your book, my Lord. That wasn't no game."

The Earl turned back to his desk and flicked over various pages of manuscript. He caught sight of the odd clever phrase, a use of words, the beautifully organised lists of maps and photographs.

All were *her* work.

A sad little smile crossed his face.

"You are quite right, Joe. Lady Tamina has a fine mind. She is a clever young woman and hard-working. I have to admit that. Indeed now the initial shock is passing, I must wish her every happiness for the future. Although I must admit I did not care for her chosen husband, Mr. Edmund Newson!"

Joe felt a shock run through him.

That name – that was the man Nancy had pointed out only a few hours ago at the Villa Mimosa, the man who had intended to sully a young woman's reputation in order to force her to marry him!

Surely it could not be the same man?

"My Lord!"

"Yes, Joe, what is it?"

"My Lord, I don't want to speak out of turn again,

and beggin' your Lordship's pardon, but I reckon Lady Tamina is in great danger!"

*

Dusk was falling when Tamina arrived at the Villa Mimosa.

Edmund helped her off the horse and hurried her indoors, hardly giving her time to stretch her limbs or to notice her surroundings.

In the cool dim hall she pulled herself away from his restricting arm.

"You must introduce me to your friends, Edmund."

"Oh, yes, certainly, Tamina. But I believe – I believe they are resting before dinner. They eat at a late hour here in Madeira. Let me show you to a room and send for your luggage."

Tamina nodded.

She was tired and aching from the jolting horseback ride in the glaring afternoon sun.

Edmund was not a good horseman. He was just too fond of using his whip and the ride had not been at all comfortable.

Although she knew she should insist on speaking to Mrs. Simmons before accepting Edmund's invitation, the thought of a cool room and a soft bed were very inviting and surely no gentlewoman would ever refuse a fellow compatriot a safe haven in a time of trouble.

Edmund ushered her upstairs, showed her into a small guest bedroom and agreed that he would send a servant to the ship for her luggage.

Tamina was hardly aware of the door closing behind him.

She flung herself onto the white bedspread and let the tears flow that she had been holding back for so long.

'Ivan, Ivan!'

She felt her heart was about to break in two.

Oh, how she loved him and there would never now be a chance to explain to him why she had cheated and pretended to be someone she was not.

Over and over again she pictured the look on his face when Edmund revealed her identity and her real name.

He had been stunned, then bewildered and finally betrayed.

And she had been the person to do that to such a good and honourable man!

Restlessly she rose and prowled around the room. This must have been a nursery at some time, she realised. There were bars on the window.

Peering out she saw that the Villa Mimosa was situated high on a hillside overlooking the harbour at Funchal.

In the distance she could see a ship heading out towards the far horizon, leaving a long wake behind, a straight white line cutting through the deep green sea.

She was certain it was the *Blue Diamond*, sailing away towards its next port of call, carrying all her hopes and dreams – *and the man she loved*.

Light faded slowly from the room and Tamina was still sitting by the window deep in thought when she realised there was a soft tapping on the door.

She crossed the room. The servant must have made good time with her trunks from the ship and she wondered what the Earl had said when they were collected.

Sighing she realised he would have had nothing to do with it. She had no doubt that he would have asked Joe to arrange to have her belongings packed and sent ashore.

"Miss Waites! Miss Waites!"

She thought she recognised the voice and wondered if she was dreaming.

"*Nancy*?"

Astonished Tamina now turned the doorknob – but nothing happened.

She realised to her horror that she was locked in the room.

"Nancy, the door will not open! What is happening? Where is Edmund?"

"Wait a moment, Miss Waites."

There was silence and Tamina pulled in vain at the door with both hands, but it was made from a huge slab of old walnut and never gave an inch.

Suddenly there was a scraping sound at the lock and after a long couple of minutes, there was a click and the door swung open.

Nancy, her bright red hair escaping from under a white lace cap, slipped into the room, her finger to her lips.

"Nancy, it is you! I cannot believe it. You have come here! Why was the door locked? How did you –?"

She held up a bent hairpin.

"Not much I ever learned from my wicked old Dad, Miss Waites, but one thing he did teach me was 'ow to pick a lock!"

Tamina's head was whirling but one thing was clear, she could no longer keep up her pretence with Nancy.

"Nancy, I am sure this will sound odd to you, but I am not Miss Tabitha Waites. My real name is actually Lady Tamina Braithwaite."

Nancy was silent for a second then smiled.

"That explains a lot that puzzled Joe and me, my Lady! You were always so well spoken, so in charge of every situation. We thought perhaps you came from gentlefolk who had fallen on 'ard times. But listen, my Lady, you 'ave to get away from this 'ouse – quickly!"

Tamina sank down on the bed, bewildered by the girl's vehement voice.

"But why? And why was the door locked? I don't understand."

The redheaded girl took a deep breath.

"It's that Mr. Newson, my Lady. He locked you in."

"What nonsense is this you are talking? Edmund? But why? He invited me to stay here with his friends, the Simmons. I accepted. There is no need to forcibly detain me."

"All I know is that the other day I overheard 'im talkin' to Mr. Simmons, saying that he was goin' to keep the girl he wanted to marry locked up 'ere in the villa for the weekend.

"She would be alone with 'im because the Simmons and their parents 'ave gone to stay with friends on the other side of the island. You would be alone with 'im, my Lady, alone without a chaperone in the 'ouse!"

Tamina gasped, her hand going to her throat.

Even in these modern times, she knew that her reputation would not survive being alone with a man for two nights.

"But does he really believe that will make me marry

him? Surely he could not believe anything so stupid? Does he think that my parents would agree, whatever the damage done to my character?"

Nancy shook her head. The ways of the gentry were beyond her.

Tamina found herself wishing desperately that the Earl was here to consult. He would know what to do.

But, of course, he was now miles away and would probably believe that she had brought this on herself when the gossip finally reached him.

Bravely she pushed her thoughts aside.

All her heartache and tears would have to wait until she was free from this ghastly situation.

"I must escape, go back to town immediately and take shelter in the Embassy," she said. "Do you know where Mr. Newson is now, Nancy?"

"Down in the study, drinkin' Mr. Simmons' prize brandy, my Lady."

"Then now is the time and quickly – you must lead the way, Nancy. Will you come with me?"

She nodded her head vigorously.

"Yes, my Lady. I 'ate it 'ere and I don't reckon you should go on your own. It's too dangerous."

And she reached over and picked up a brass candlestick from the bedside table.

Tamina smiled.

Nancy looked so fierce clutching her weapon.

They would not need to resort to violence, she was quite certain. She was sure that Edmund was not dangerous. Heavens, he had been her fiancé until recently! Misguided and wicked, yes, but dangerous?

134

That was ridiculous.

And with Nancy behind her, she opened the door and began to creep down the stairs.

They had just reached the hall when a door crashed open and Edmund appeared.

"Tamina! Where do you think you are going?"

"Edmund! I have no idea what your silly plan is for me, but I refuse to stay here a second longer. I am going back to Funchal and to the British Embassy!"

Edmund's face went bright scarlet with rage and to Tamina's astonishment, he stepped forward and grasped her by her shoulders.

"Oh, no, my good lady, you are not! You are staying here with me for the whole weekend. And if you will not stay voluntarily and agree to marry me, then you will stay under duress, but you will still end up as my wife!"

Tamina struggled to escape but his hands were too strong and she cried out as his fingers bit into her soft flesh.

She was powerless to stop him forcing her back up the stairs when suddenly there was a cry, a thud and his hands fell away.

Tamina turned, pushing her tangled locks from her cheeks.

Edmund lay groaning at her feet and Nancy stood over him, still holding the heavy candlestick she had used to knock him senseless.

"Nancy! What have you done? Is he dead?"

"Dead? No worse luck, not this one, my Lady. His skull is far too thick! But quickly, we must run. He will come round very soon. So hurry, my Lady, we must escape!"

CHAPTER TEN

Tamina stood in shock for a second or two, staring down at where Edmund lay moaning at her feet. There was blood in his fair hair showing the spot where Nancy had hit him.

She knew this man, whom she had once thought she loved, had been very determined to trap her into a forced marriage, but she still felt badly at leaving another human being in pain.

But Nancy was pulling at her arm and Tamina shook herself out of her guilt.

Her first responsibility was to get herself and Nancy away from this place.

Hopefully one of the other servants would be sure to find Edmund soon and help him.

"Quickly, my Lady. Oh, do hurry!"

Tamina followed Nancy down a long tiled corridor and out through the kitchen, ignoring the startled looks of two cooks busy working at the stove.

"We must go back into Funchal town," said Tamina as they ran across the courtyard and out of a gate that led to an orchard. "I shall go to the Embassy immediately and tell them what has been happening."

"But we cannot go by the road, my Lady. That

wicked man 'as an 'orse and will catch us easy as easy. Oh, I do wish my Joe was here. He'd know what to do."

"I fear Joe and the Earl are heading out to sea at this very moment," grunted Tamina as they hurried through the trees.

It was hot and humid under the leafy branches and for a second she longed for the cool sea breezes she had grown used to on board ship.

She could not say so out loud, but she wished as fervently as Nancy that the man *she* loved was by her side to help her.

Suddenly Nancy winced, stumbled and wailed as she caught her foot on a large root and turned her ankle.

"Oohh!"

"Nancy! Oh, what has happened? Are you all right? Can you walk?"

Nancy fought hard to hold back the tears that were starting to brim in her eyes. The pain in her ankle was awful, but she was not going to tell Lady Tamina how bad it felt.

She leant against a tree trunk to catch her breath.

"I turned my ankle over. Yes, it was bad for a second, but now 'tis better. But perhaps you should go on without me, my Lady. You'll be a sight faster alone."

Tamina looked shocked. She had been brought up listening and learning stories of honour and courage told to her by her father and brothers.

She recognised she could never abandon Nancy to Edmund's anger.

"Nonsense!" she urged briskly, inspecting the ankle, which was swelling even as she looked. It would need a bandage of some sort.

Without thinking twice she ripped the sleeve from her white dress, which was now sadly dirty and tied it tightly round Nancy's foot.

"There! That should help. Now Nancy. Lean on me and we will get along very well. Look – we are nearly at the end of the orchard. I do believe that is the cliff top in front of us. We are sure to find a path there leading down to Funchal."

She was right.

Half-carrying the limping Nancy, Tamina left the shelter of the trees and came out onto the grassy cliff top.

The humid atmosphere vanished immediately and Tamina took a deep breath of the fresh breeze blowing in from the Atlantic.

It was early evening now and the hot sun glowing orange was dropping down through the aquamarine sky towards the far horizon.

Tamina wondered if the Earl was standing on the deck of the *Blue Diamond* watching the sun set and cursing the day he had decided to employ Miss Tabitha Waites as his secretary.

Even as she and Nancy stumbled over the short turf, Tamina could think of nothing else but the Earl.

Even Edmund's perfidy faded into the background of her mind.

But suddenly her thoughts were rudely interrupted as Nancy gulped.

"My Lady, listen, there's an 'orse comin'! I can 'ear the 'oof beats."

The two girls stopped and turned.

With a sinking heart Tamina realised that Nancy was right.

A horseman was indeed riding at full gallop across the turf towards them. She could see the blood on his face – it was Edmund Newson!

*

The Earl and Joe had left the *Blue Diamond* seconds before it set sail on the next leg of its journey.

The gangway had actually been lifting from the pier when the Earl raced down it, his face grim, his dark hair flying and with Joe close on his heels.

A flying leap off the end of the gangway had landed them on the dockside, ignoring the alarmed cries and angry shouts of the sailors and workers around them.

A handful of sovereigns were thrown at the driver of an open carriage who was waiting for customers to be taken up the steep slope to Reids Hotel.

"Villa Mimosa, as fast as you can!" the Earl snapped in Portuguese and only wished he could have taken the reins himself. "There's another guinea in it for you if you make this old buggy fly!"

"You are quite certain that is where Newson said he would take his kidnapped victim?" he asked Joe.

He could hardly speak the words.

Tamina *kidnapped*!

She was in such danger and only now could he admit to himself that he still loved her.

Whether she was Tabitha Waites or Lady Tamina Braithwaite, she was his dearest, darling girl and he would do anything in his power to save her.

The young valet nodded not having the breath to reply. He was terrified, clinging to the rough sides of the swaying carriage as it careered through the narrow cobbled streets of Funchal.

He glanced sideways at the Earl's angry dark face and felt a twinge of pity for Edmund Newson.

He would not want to be in that gentleman's shoes when the Earl caught up with him!

The sun was beginning to drop down the sky when they reached the Villa Mimosa. The wide iron gates were standing open and the carriage careered up the long drive, gravel flying from the horse's hooves and ground to a halt outside the ornate front porch.

Joe saw gold change hands once more and next the Earl was battering on the huge studded door.

"Tamina! *Tamina*! Are you there? Answer me! It's Ivan! Don't be scared. I've come to fetch you."

But there was no reply and the door was firmly locked.

"I know where the kitchen entrance is, my Lord."

"Quickly then, Joe. Lead the way."

But as they both hurried around the villa, he felt a growing dread creeping through him. What would they find?

He was beginning to doubt Newson's sanity and a madman could not be trusted.

Tamina would surely have struggled. Would he have hurt her in some way in trying to restrain her?

The Earl knew he would never rest again if that monster had inflicted pain on his beloved.

A hasty word with a servant in the kitchen sent the two men running from the courtyard out through the orchard towards the cliffs beyond.

"Why did they come this way, my Lord?" gasped Joe. "Why not 'ead for town?"

The Earl quickened his stride.

The servant had made it quite clear that the girls had fled from the house. And they had both looked frightened – as if all the demons of hell were after them.

"The kitchen boy said that Newson left the house on horseback just after Lady Tamina and Nancy fled. I would expect that Lady Tamina realised he could easily catch them if they stayed on the road. She would have had her wits about her, even though she was scared."

Suddenly, as they hurried through the trees, the Earl stopped, bent down and picked up something caught on a low bush.

"Look! This piece of muslin – the yellow and white pattern – I believe it has been torn from Lady Tamina's dress."

The Earl raised it to his lips. He could smell the faint aroma of lavender and rose – the perfume that his beloved girl wore.

Joe frowned.

"I reckon they've used a piece of the lady's dress as some sort of bandage, my Lord. So – one of them has been hurt in some way!"

And with a look that said more than words ever could, they both broke into a run, heading for the cliff tops in front of them, dreading what they would find there.

*

Tamina stood with her arm round Nancy as Edmund cantered up.

There was a trickle of blood on his forehead, but it was the mad soulless glare in his eyes that frightened her the most.

She knew that there was nowhere to run, but was

determined to fight and show him she was not afraid.

He swung out of the saddle and strode towards her.

"So, my sweetheart, did you find my hospitality so abhorrent? I can assure you that when you have spent the weekend in my company, you will be only too *delighted* to be my fiancée once again."

Tamina's blue eyes blazed.

"Edmund! Have you lost your wits? Do you think you can keep me locked up like some – some slave girl? Are you living fifty years ago in the last century? This is ridiculous."

"You say that now, Tamina, my love, but you will think differently *very soon*!"

"My Lady, 'e 'as gone mad!" whispered Nancy. "Look at 'is eyes. We 'ad a dog like that once. My old Dad 'ad to destroy it!"

Tamina raised his head defiantly.

"Edmund, think what you are doing. Lord Daventry will inquire as to my whereabouts. He is not the sort of man you would wish to have as your enemy."

Edmund laughed – and it was a cold callous laugh.

"The Earl, your would-be rescuer, is far out to sea by now. He is of no use to you at all. Indeed he seemed to almost have a dislike for you when we met in the town earlier. What can you have done to upset him, my sweet?

"So it is no use calling for him to help you. Anyway these book-writing aristocrats possess no backbone or courage when it is a matter of a hand-to-hand fight. They are only of use when ordinary men are in the front lines in battle, fighting and dying at their commands."

"What rubbish you speak, Edmund. Ivan is worth a hundred like you."

"Oh, it is *Ivan* now, is it?"

He swayed violently and his expression grew even wilder.

"So perhaps your innocent air is not as genuine as you would have everyone believe!"

As Tamina groaned, the colour rushing into her face as the meaning of his insult reached her, Nancy suddenly limped forward and launched herself in a fury at Edmund.

"You 'orrible wicked man! Speakin' like that of 'er Ladyship. You should be ashamed of yourself!"

She flung herself at him, her little fists battering at his chest.

Edmund laughed and fended off her attack, then took two steps backwards as her onslaught grew fiercer.

Nancy was only slim, but she had been born and bred in the roughest area of London and had learnt to fight on the streets as soon as she could walk.

Edmund yelled as the young girl's nails found his face and he roughly grabbed her arms and tried to shake her free.

But she clung on like a terrier with a rat.

They both staggered sideways and then with a curse Edmund flung Nancy away from him.

"Watch out!"

Tamina raced forward as she realised with a great rush of fear that Nancy was swaying right on the cliff edge, hundreds of feet above the jagged rocks that speared upwards out of the sea.

Nancy tried to find her balance, but her sprained ankle gave way under her.

Tamina clasped her hand and pulled her forwards,

but as she turned, the ground crumbled under her feet.

With the last inch of her strength she pushed Nancy to safety as she herself slid over the edge.

And as she tried to stop herself falling, her hands scrabbling at the loose earth of the cliff, she thought she heard the sound of a struggle and the Earl's voice calling out in despair,

"*Tamina*!"

Tamina now slid down the crumbling cliff face, screaming as she struggled to find a foothold, a handhold, something to stop her falling hundreds of feet into the sea.

Suddenly her toes hit a thin hard ledge and there to her left was a gnarled root sticking out from the earth and mud.

She clung to it and realised that her headlong fall had stopped.

She gazed upwards and to her joy the Earl's dear face appeared over the edge of the cliff.

"Tamina! My darling girl. Oh, dear Heavens! Do not move. Not an inch."

"Ivan! You came back for me."

"Did you think I would ever leave you? This is all my fault. Oh! – "

Tamina gave a little cry as the root began to ease out of the mud.

"*Ivan*!"

But he had vanished.

Tamina stood as still as she could refusing to look down at the wicked rocks and crashing waves far below.

Even in this time of desperation, part of her heart was singing with joy. He had called her his *darling girl*!

He must have forgiven her for misleading him.

Her feelings for him were returned!

He loved her! Even if her life was about to end, she knew that she would know the meaning of ecstatic joy in these last few moments.

"Tamina!"

The Earl was back, leaning precariously over the edge. In his hands he held the bridle off Edmund's horse, the long reins still attached.

"Listen, dear one, I am going to lower the bridle down to you. You will need to catch it and then let go of the root and hold it with both hands."

"Ivan – ! "

Tamina felt a great rush of terror.

"I know – but you must trust me. Joe and I will pull you up. It will hurt your poor arms and shoulders – I will not lie to you. But we can only do it if you trust me. Do you?"

She stared up into the dark eyes she had come to love so much.

The Earl's face was now white and tense, already streaked with dirt. He had cast off his jacket and was leaning out over the edge, the leather bridle in his strong capable hands.

"*I trust you – with my life – forever*!"

And a look of great love passed wordlessly between them.

The Earl dropped the bridle slowly down the cliff and Tamina spluttered as streams of dirt and small stones spattered onto her face.

She could see that the end of one rein was twisted

round his wrist and she guessed Joe held the other one.

Now the bridle was two feet above her head and she realised with a sinking heart that it was as far as it would reach.

She would need to stretch right above her head to catch it with one hand and that would mean letting go of the root that was the only support holding her upright.

On top of the cliff Joe was lying flat out next to the Earl, gripping the end of the thin leather straps with all his might.

"They're a bit too short, my Lord," he muttered desperately. "Lady Tamina will never be able to reach the bridle. No young lady could."

The Earl blinked and then recognised the words that came immediately to his mind as the truth.

"Believe me, Joe. This young lady can – and *will*!"

Tamina took a deep breath and closed her eyes.

For a long moment the cliff, the swirling air and the perilous fall beneath her – all vanished.

She was eight years old and she had followed her two big brothers, Peter and Guy, to the fast flowing river than run through the Braithwaite estate in Devon, insisting she was old enough to play with them.

Jeering they had made her tuck her petticoats in her bloomers and then forced her to jump from rock to rock across the deep rapids.

One of them had always been just behind her waiting to catch her if she slipped, but it had not made the jumps any easier. And she had learnt to be brave, to take chances and to trust in those she loved.

Now she opened her eyes, took a deep breath and gazed up into the Earl's loving eyes.

If this was to be her last sight on this dear earth, then she wanted nothing more.

Letting go of the root she jumped feeling the ledge give way beneath the pressure of her feet.

For a second she hung there, then her hands tangled in the straps of the bridle and the Earl and Joe grunted as they took the full weight on the reins.

The leather cut cruelly into Tamina's wrists and she bit her lip to stop crying out.

She hung in mid air, felt both her shoes fall off and go tumbling down to the rocks below.

Next the two men were hauling her up, up, over the edge of the cliff onto the turf and into the Earl's strong waiting arms.

For long minutes neither spoke.

He cradled Tamina against his chest, kissing the red weals the reins had cut into her delicate wrists.

"Edmund – ?" she mumbled.

The Earl's voice was harsh and cold.

"Gone and to the devil, I do hope. He'll *never* dare show his cowardly face in England again."

He brushed the tangled golden curls back from her face.

"Tamina, my darling girl. I thought I had lost you! I thought my stupid pride had cost me all I hold most dear in the world."

He shuddered.

"You will never know the curses I brought onto my own head when I heard about that scoundrel Newson and his wicked plans for you.

"I should have listened when you tried to tell me

what had happened to make you pretend to be someone you were not."

She smiled up at him – all her courage and love for him shining out of her eyes.

"My pride caused me as much trouble as yours, Ivan. If I had not been so much concerned with my own feelings, I would have told you right away who I was. That I wanted to run away from England and a man who had no honour.

"But then I would never have had the chance of travelling with you and falling in love. I never stopped trusting you. As soon as I heard your voice, I knew I was safe, my Lord."

"No! Not my Lord. It must be Ivan and Tamina from now on."

He brushed his lips across her forehead.

Tamina felt her heart swell with happiness.

She was not aware of Joe and Nancy standing a few yards away, hand in hand, or that the brief Madeira sunset had given way to night.

She was only aware of the Earl's dark eyes gazing down at her, full of the passionate love she had always longed for.

She smiled and his heart jumped at the beauty of her lips.

Even bedraggled and dirty with scratches across her cheeks and dark bruises on her hands, she was the most glorious creature he had ever seen.

"Are you certain you would not prefer me to be Miss Tabitha Waites? After all, that is who you fell in love with, not Lady Tamina Braithwaite!"

He laughed softly.

"Miss Tabitha Waites was indeed a very determined and opinionated young woman! Yes, I fell in love with her. Probably from the first time I saw her, when she was wearing that ridiculous green hat!"

Tamina nestled closer to him, glorying in the feel of his strong arms encircling her.

Mischievously she replied,

"It's a great pity you did not fall in love with Lady Tamina when you first saw her! In fact I have the distinct memory that at the Mercer's ball, you thought I was an impudent youngster, who should have been tucked up in bed and not annoying her elders and betters on the dance floor!"

The Earl gasped and frowned.

Then, as he gazed into her laughing sapphire eyes, he realised to his astonishment that, yes, this was the elfin bird of paradise who had first told him of Lady Eunice's treachery on that fateful night!

"When did you realise we had met before?" he asked in delight.

Tamina smiled.

"I kept thinking I had seen your face somewhere before, but it was not until you peered over the top of the cliff that it came back to me!"

He ran his fingers tenderly over the scratches on her cheek.

"So when I ask your father for your dear hand in marriage, I can in all honesty say that we have known each other for a little longer than I had thought!"

The expression on Tamina's face changed to one of deepest devotion.

"I love my parents and would never wish to hurt

them in any way. But, even if they refused permission, I will marry you, Ivan. You are my soulmate, the man I have longed for in my dreams. I love you with all my mind, body and being."

"Then our dreams are identical, Tamina, my dearest sweetheart. I love you with all my heart and soul too and know that I shall wait impatiently for the day when I can claim you as my wife!"

And so saying, he bent his head to claim her with a kiss that confirmed once and forever the love they shared.

*

Three months later to the day, just before Christmas, a wedding took place in the parish church of Braithwaite, the village that nestled in the folds of the Devon hills, part of the vast Braithwaite estate.

Snow lay on the ground decorating the trees and gardens, but the sky was a liquid blue and a pale sun was shining brightly on all the guests who had gathered to celebrate this much acclaimed marriage, the joining of two great families.

St. Anselm's Church was decorated with branches of greenery and beautiful white lilies. Little circlets of holly hung from the ends of the pews, the scarlet berries making a splash of colour in the soft candlelight.

Elegant in grey silk and lace, the family emeralds gleaming at her neck, Tamina's mother, escorted by her two sons on special leave from the Services, made her way slowly down the aisle, smiling acknowledgement at those gathered to witness her daughter's joy.

Representatives from all the great families of the land were present.

The Lord and Lady Mercer and Mary-Rose their

daughter. The Duke and Duchess of Marlow whose daughter Charlotte was to be Tamina's bridesmaid. Countess Lichley, Tamina's elderly Godmother.

They all mingled with the local gentry and the staff from the Braithwaite and Daventry estates.

Tamina and the Earl had also invited two very special guests.

Sitting proudly in a pew near the front of the Church, Mr. and Mrs. Joe Goodall waited hand in hand for the ceremony to begin.

Nancy, resplendent in amber velvet, her bright red hair swept up under a concoction of feathers and lace, kept glancing down at the shiny gold ring on the third finger of her left hand.

She did not reckon that anyone could be as happy as she was today. As Lady Tamina's maid she would now be working alongside her Joe once their Master and Mistress were wed.

She could still see the look on her old Dad's face when she had told him. As the old saying went – worth a pound of cherries – that had been!

Standing at the altar, Ivan, the Earl of Daventry, was trying hard not to fidget. He was not nervous, but what was taking her so long?

Just then the organ music swelled to a crescendo and he turned to see a vision in shining white silk and lace coming towards him on the arm of her father. A long veil like a cloud of winter snow trailed behind her supported on her golden head by the famous Braithwaite diamond tiara.

She had refused to have the veil cover her face and, as he watched, the Earl could see the smile he loved so much blaze up at him.

As he reached for her hand, his fingers warmly squeezing hers, Tamina felt a wave of love and adoration sweep over her and she thanked God for seeing her through all the trials and tribulations they had shared on land and sea and bringing her to safe harbour.

"I will love you forever, my darling Tamina, into Eternity and beyond," he whispered against her veil, "I feel I must have waited a million years for this glorious moment."

"I love and adore you, Ivan, and this wonderful day will live in my consciousness for all my life. My love for you knows no limits and will last and last and you have made me the happiest woman in the world."

For the love they shared was not a hidden one, but was there for all to share, joining them as man and wife, together and forever.

Then as the Parson approached them, they were lifted up by the beauty and wonder of their feelings for each other to the celestial glory of the Kingdom of Love.